THE
GHOST MAN

By Malcolm Haslett

This book is dedicated to the memory of my mother.

1

A woman struggled up the rain-spattered road out of the village, fighting to make headway against the fierce gale coming in off the North Atlantic. Now and then she would grimace and risk a glance into the driving rain, out over the turbulent grey waters of the ocean. There was nothing in that direction but mile upon mile of tumbling waves, driving relentlessly towards the rocky shore. Out beyond the Further Foreland, where the forbidding mass of Slieve Trascart plunged almost vertically into the stormy sea, a single shaft of bright sunlight cut through the lowering cloud, and for several minutes it turned the churning waves into a pool of splendid light. But then it was gone, surrendering to the uncompromising roar of the waves and the wind, and the day sank back into an all-pervading greyness.

A further squall hit her as she reached the corner. Clutching at the hood of her raincoat, she pulled it down over her forehead to give her shelter from the heavy, stinging drops. Her clear, well-proportioned face, too old to be called pretty, too young to be thought wise, was already ruddy from the combined effects of wind and rain.

Then she was round the bend, with her back to the storm.

That was when she looked up across the inlet towards the Near Foreland. This was a low headland to the west of the village, jutting defiantly out into the tossing water of the ocean. Her eyes were drawn to the grim old house which stood there alone at the top of the ridge. Its walls were of the same grey stone as the cliffs which lined the headland, but otherwise the angular symmetry of the house did not fit well with its surroundings. There was something defiantly deliberate about its structured gables, a statement of human will against the stark background of the tumbledown rock of the cliffs, the haphazard lumpy knolls of the Foreland itself and the scattered bushes which struggled for survival among them.

That house had been empty for as long as she could remember. But to her surprise she now saw that there was a car sheltering in its lee, and a van beside it, parked among the stunted apple trees which were all that was left of its orchard. And as she watched, two figures emerged from the house. It was hard to see from this distance, but they appeared to shake hands, struggling to keep upright in the wind, before one of them was almost swept along by the gale to the door of the van. A moment or two later he was driving off down the rutted lane towards the road. The other man turned and climbed very deliberately, almost as if fighting against more than the wind, back up the steps into the gaunt old house.

'So someone has bought it!' she thought with surprise. And they're moving in already. She wondered if they knew the house's reputation. Many years ago it had belonged to an Englishman, a doctor, some said. And he had died, she had never heard exactly how, during the Troubles at the time of independence. Ever since then it had been seen as an unlucky house, a place of ill omen. Those who had tried to live in it, they said, never stayed long.

She had now reached the top of the inlet separating Killoole village from the Near Foreland. Here, some way from the village centre, was the post office and general store run by Maeve Meahan. It nestled into the hillside as if it were part of the earth itself. This was the woman's destination. As she pushed the door open she was greeted by a cracked and tinny sound at the back of the shop, the sound of a metal bell grown tired over decades of welcoming customers. A thin woman of about fifty, with sharp, accusing eyes, came out of the back room.

"Who is it, Maeve, that's moving into the big house?" asked the newcomer, pulling back her dripping hood. "I didn't think anyone would ever live there again. And it's not even in good repair. I'm sure that roof has been letting in rain for years."

"It's even stranger than you think, Kathleen," said Maeve. The post-mistress liked to give the impression she was always ahead of everyone with the news. And she usually was. "It's a single man. Tall fellow. And they say he's from the North." This she had heard from Mrs. O'Donnell just five minutes previously.

"From the North? Why has he come down here then? Who is he, do they know?"

Maeve shrugged. Mrs. O'Donnell had provided no information on these points. "There are quite a few people from the North coming to these parts now to buy up holiday homes," she said vaguely.

Kathleen frowned. "That old place is hardly a holiday home. The holiday homes are all further north or east. We've never had any in Killoole before…"

"Wait till you see," said Maeve confidently. "He'll be down here in a week or two with his family, trying to make it as spick and span as you like…"

The hollow clank of the bell made them both turn towards the doorway. A tall figure in a raincoat was entering, stooping slightly under the low threshold. They watched expectantly, but when he straightened up they saw it was only Father Brian, the young parish priest who had himself arrived in the village some six months before.

"Afternoon, ladies," he said brightly, his ruddy, wind-blown face twisting into a rather forced smile. "Terrible weather you have up here!"

"Straight down from Iceland, they say," said Maeve almost gleefully. "You must have done something awful in a previous life, father, for to be sent to a place like this!"

"I'm not sure your theology is very sound there, Mrs. Meahan," said the priest jovially. He was the only one in the village who called her by her surname. "We believe in an after-life, not an eternal circle, as they do in eastern religions…"

She looked at him coyly, and it wasn't clear whether she was mocking him or just engaging in friendly banter. "But when you look at the state we're all in," she said, "you need some way of explaining why it's all going downhill, surely…"

He didn't seem keen to continue this theme. "Could I have three aerogrammes?" he said quietly.

As Maeve fished in the desk for the aerogrammes, Kathleen asked:

"Do you know anything, Father, about the man moving in at the old house?"

The young priest looked surprised.

"I hadn't heard about that! You mean that empty old place on the headland? What do they call it - the 'Bastion'? Are you sure?"

"Saw him myself just ten minutes ago," she said. "Came with a van. A small van, but it looked as if he might have been moving in furniture."

Father Brian looked put out, vexed that someone else always seemed to know such things before he did.

"Well, no doubt we'll find out who he is pretty soon. News doesn't take long to travel in this part of the world…" And he smiled blandly at Maeve as she gave him the aerogrammes and his change.

"I'm sure you're right there, Father," murmured Maeve Meahan as the tall frame moved awkwardly back towards the door. The hollow bell jangled above the counter, and a moment later the priest had disappeared back into the gale.

Kathleen moved around the shop, collecting her purchases. Maeve watched her, and as she brought her basket back to the counter, the coy look had returned to the shopkeeper's face.

"How's your boy Tony these days, Kathleen?" she asked.

Kathleen looked up at her sharply. "Oh, he's fine, he's fine," she murmured softly, opening her purse.

But her eyes took on a vacant expression, and looked past Maeve at the cigarette packs lining the wall behind her.

The truth was she had not seen her twelve-year old son Tony since early that morning, and she had no idea where he was.

2

Tony tripped and fell. Luckily he fell on a grassy spot among the rocks and was only winded. He picked himself up, soaked to the skin. His glasses had fallen off, but he found them without too much trouble and they weren't broken. He put them back on, but everything was blurred, so he did what he could to dry them by wiping them on his sleeve.

The others had disappeared. He stared round hopelessly, trying to work out which way they could have gone. He was determined not to lose them. He was also determined not to cry. He knew that if he did they would only laugh at him all the more. So he wiped his glasses again and rubbed the knee which had taken the brunt of his fall. And then trundled off through the rocks in pursuit of Shamie's gang.

That's what they called them in the village. There were two 'gangs' in Killoole, Shamie's and Dominic's. They weren't really gangs, in the sense that there were no street fights or anything like that. They simply roved round the village and the shoreline on either side of it, chattering and throwing stones into the sea, and ignoring each other for the most part. All of the children in the village, nevertheless, seemed to gravitate sooner or later to one group or the other. And Tony had decided long ago that he belonged to Shamie's little band. There weren't so many of them, but they seemed to do more interesting things. They wandered further from the village and had far more exciting hideouts. And Shamie, tall and lean for his sixteen years, was much more impressive than Dominic, the butcher's son, who was squat and ugly and looked like a pit-bull. It was Shamie himself who had won Tony's loyalty. He was three or four years older, and always wore such a confident look. Shamie had a way about him. He could sit there and just talk to the others and hold their attention in a way that Mr. O'Connell or Miss McGinn at the primary school could never have done. Shamie was full of stories, about far off places where wars were being fought, a place called Palestine where they were fighting for liberty and a place called Congo where black people were killing each other. And Shamie always had explanations for why these things were happening.

He said it was mostly because of the bad things the colonialists had done hundreds of years ago, particularly the British.

Shamie could also tell stories about the old days, here in Ireland…

Shamie, what's more, had protected Tony. The lad was an easy target for mockery. Because he had glasses and spiky hair and a snub nose. Because he was ugly, or so Shelagh McKeever said. And because he was stupid…

He knew he was stupid. He had always known, even though his mother would never let anyone say it. He had his own ways, his mother said. He's different, but don't call him stupid. He had never seen his mother so angry as when she caught Shelagh McKeever calling him an idiot and spitting at him. His mother had grabbed Shelagh by the pullover and given her a hard smack round the back of the head. That was why Shelagh was now the worst at calling him names, like "eedgit" and "cretin" and "moron".

But Shamie had protected him. Well, he did it a few times anyway. "Give over, Shelagh," he would say. "Leave the cub alone. Can't you see he's crying."

…Tony looked round in panic. He couldn't see the others anywhere. They'd gone and left him again on purpose, alone on the shore, in the middle of a rainstorm.

Should he go on after them? He wasn't even sure they'd gone any further. Just as likely they had turned back towards the village. He began to feel afraid. If he stayed too long on the shore the sea might come in and cut off his way home. That's what the other children had told him, and he wasn't totally sure they'd been teasing. His mother had once scolded him for staying out on the shore by himself. There were some 'bad characters' about, she said. But when he'd asked the others about these bad characters they had only laughed.

"There's a big, bad giant lives on Slieve Trascart," Shelagh had taunted him. "And he'll come and eat you!" And she arched herself above him and made a gobbling noise.

Tony wouldn't have minded Shelagh's teasing now, just so long as there'd been somebody with him. He was moving as swiftly as he could back along the shore towards the village, clambering over the rocky bits, trotting over the short stretches of sand. To add to his misery it was beginning to grow dark.

They had come quite a long way, he knew. But he had been concentrating on listening to the others chatter and hadn't realised quite how far. He turned one headland, hoping to see the village. But instead there was a small inlet, and through the driving rain he made out another low headland at the far side. For a moment he panicked. Had he somehow made a mistake? Was he going the wrong way? Surely not… Had the shoreline somehow changed? Had some magician come along and played a nasty trick on him, putting the sea on the wrong side?

It was getting ever darker, and the rain was getting heavier. He hurried on. Finally he turned the second headland.

And then he saw the others. Across the final inlet before the village. At least he thought it was them. Several figures, blurred in the rain and barely visible in the gathering gloom, scuttling up across the field just below the big house, the old house on the Near Foreland where nobody usually went.

He broke into a run, but once again slipped on the wet rocks and fell. This time it took him several minutes to find his glasses.

The rain was now pelting down, and by the time he reached the bottom of the slope below the grim old house Tony was exhausted. He was also soaked to the skin. And uncomfortable. The wet sand he had picked up when he fell had wormed its way into his clothes. It had also got on to his glasses, and no matter how hard he rubbed them against his sweater he couldn't get them clean.

He reached the bottom of the slope beneath the big house. He felt so completely miserable that he was tempted just to go straight home, to the warmth of the kitchen and of his mother. But some spark of pride prevented him. He wanted to catch up with Shamie and the gang, just to prove to them he wasn't as stupid as they thought.

He started to climb the steep grassy slope.

As he climbed, he looked up at the gaunt edifice above. There was still enough light for its high chimneys and gables to form a jagged pattern against the grey, windswept sky. The old house, he had heard, was haunted.

Someone, they said, had been killed there. That was why very few people, not even the two gangs, ever went near it.

Yet he went on climbing.

There were steps now, stone steps half covered by the long grass. He followed them, one by one, concentrating, making sure he didn't trip.

Finally the steps ended, and he found himself on a wide area of plain concrete, glistening dully in the wet. Immediately above him loomed the intimidating shape of the house.

Tentatively Tony advanced into the dark, wet yard. To his left was a ramshackle old shed of some sort. To the right was the house itself, rearing high above him.

He glanced nervously at its walls, grey and glistening in the rain. He could hear the rain gurgling gently in some hidden drain. Directly above where he stood was a tall window. It had coloured glass and was, he thought, a bit like the window at the far end of the chapel, behind the altar.

He inched nervously forward, his eyes glued to the window, fascinated. When he came close to it, he saw the light.

Through the misted, coloured glass of the window he could just make out the dull outlines of a great empty hall, with what looked like a staircase to one side. The light was no more than a dull glow, somewhere in the middle of the house, beyond the hall itself. It reflected faintly on the heavy woodwork of the staircase and the large pictures hanging on the walls around it.

And then, even as he peered through the window, it began to grow stronger.

The boy felt the hairs rise on his head.

"Tony!" came a ghostly whisper from behind him.

He whipped round and saw that it was Shamie, beckoning to him from the door of the broken-down shed.

"Come here, Tony, before they see you!"

He needed no further bidding. In a flash he was in through the door past Shamie, into the shelter of the hut.

Someone switched on a torch, and Tony saw they were all there, Kieran and Shelagh and Marie and Liam, and several others he couldn't see properly, perched on an assortment of packing cases and discarded timber. One or two of them giggled, but Tony didn't care. He was safe, back with the gang.

Shamie crossed to the other side of the hut and took his place in an old armchair. Tony saw that Kieran, the next oldest after Shamie, was on the gang leader's right, slouched on a rolled-up carpet with a cigarette planted ostentatiously in his mouth. He now pulled noisily on it, and Tony saw the smoke rise slowly from his mouth up past a shelf lined with what looked like paint pots. There were also several old bottles of liquid, some clear and some a pale purplish colour. Tony had some notion that these were things that might catch fire, but Kieran didn't seem to care, so maybe he knew better.

From his chair Shamie pointed to a battered old suitcase near the door.

"Sit there, Tony," he said. Then he took the torch from Kieran and switched it off.

Tony stumbled in the dark towards where he had seen the suitcase and literally fell on top of it. Adjusting himself to a sitting position, he turned towards the spot where he guessed Shamie was sitting.

"Wha… what's the light, the light in the house?" he asked breathlessly.

"It's ghosts, you gawbeen," Shelagh's voice came out of the dark, melodramatically deep and scary. "It's the ghosts of the people who were killed here, come back to take their revenge… And they'll be looking for the ones who are too stupid to get away from them, Tony… Ones like you!"

"Shut up, Shelagh," said Shamie from his imperial throne in the darkness. "Leave the cub alone… You've never been here before, Tony, have you? We only come here every so often. But this is our most secret hideout, one that Dominic and his gang will never get to know about…"

"No, I never came near this house before," said Tony.

"You were too scared of the ghosts, weren't you?" said Shelagh in a trembling voice.

"Give over, Shelagh." This time it was Kieran who interrupted her. "But seriously, Shamie, what are we going to do about the man coming to live in the house here? This is the greatest hideout we ever had. But we can hardly go on meeting here now..."

"Unless..." said Shamie. And he turned the torch back on. It glowed dramatically on his face.

They all waited expectantly. "Unless what?" asked Marie finally. "Unless what, Shamie?"

Shamie seemed to have spoken before he knew what he was going to say. But finally he finished his sentence.

"Unless we can drive him out again!"

"Drive him out?" asked Liam, who was the next youngest after Tony. "How would we drive him out, Tony?"

"I haven't thought of that yet," said Shamie. "I'm still thinking about it..."

"And why should we drive him out, anyway?" said Marie. "Sure the house belongs to him now."

There was a short silence.

"Who is he, anyway?" Liam asked.

"He's a priest in disguise, come to exorcise these haunted walls," intoned Shelagh, and laughed at the thought.

"He's not, is he?" asked Tony.

There were one or two impatient noises in the dark, and Shelagh tittered.

"He couldn't be a priest," said Shamie abruptly. "I heard he was a Protestant."

This was greeted with a silence.

"Nah....," said Kieran sceptically. "Why should a Protestant come here?"

"My Mam said he was from the North," said Kieran, "but that doesn't mean he's a Protestant. There are plenty of Catholics in the North."

"I know he's a Protestant," said Shamie confidently.

"How?" they all challenged him.

"He hasn't gone to mass yet, and the priest didn't even know he'd moved in."

"That doesn't mean anything," Kieran retorted. "Sure there are lots of people don't go to mass these days…"

"You just wait and see. He's a Protestant, all right, believe you me."

There was a faint noise from the direction of the house. It sounded like a door being closed, ever so deliberately and carefully. Shamie switched off the torch. A moment later a bright light went on in the room opposite the hut's window.

Several of them moved towards the window and peered out. There was a man in the room opposite, not fifteen yards from them across the yard.

He was a tall man with greying hair. He seemed to be leaning over a sink. They heard the noise of water pouring into a kettle.

"He's making tea," whispered Liam.

"So Protestants drink tea too," said Shelagh in a low voice, and began sniggering so hard that she fell off the bench where she was perched, with a clatter.

The light went out in the big house.

They crouched in a tense silence, waiting for something to happen.

"Do you think he heard us?" whispered Tony.

Nobody answered. And from the house there came only an ominous silence. It was some time before anyone spoke again. Then it was Shelagh who said:

"Maybe he's not a real person at all. Maybe he's… a ghost."

She had probably meant this as a joke, but her voice didn't have its usual confident ring.

Kieran the sceptic made an impatient noise.

"Don't talk nonsense, Shelagh. There's no such thing as ghosts."

"But really," Shelagh insisted. "There were people killed in there once, my Granny told me. She remembers it. So maybe... maybe this is one of their ghosts, come back to occupy the house and haunt it."

This time it was Shamie who intervened.

"That's enough, Shelagh. Keep your nonsense to yourself. You'll be giving the others nightmares..."

"She'll be giving herself nightmares too," said Kieran scornfully.

Silence descended again on the small company. Tony, perched on his suitcase, suddenly began to shiver.

3

The mist floated dismally across the wet, deserted bog, restricting visibility to a few hundred feet in every direction. The tufted heather was dissected by a narrow strip of rough tarmac. Unlike most Irish roads, this one was straight as a die. But what it lacked in curves it made up for in humps and hollows. One hillock was more pronounced than the others, and here someone had dug a small quarry out of the rock. This now served as a rough parking space, difficult to spot from the road until you were right on top of it.

Mahood had been parked here for twenty minutes or more. From the driving seat he could see a fair way along the road to the east, and it was in this direction that he kept glancing, impatiently tapping the steering wheel with his index finger, to the rhythm - he realised with some surprise - of a hymn tune he had not heard, let alone sung, for many years. One of those tunes his father used to hammer out on Sunday evenings on the piano in the front room, while the rest of the family retreated as far as they could into various corners of the house.

McFaul was late. They had agreed to meet at six, and it was now almost half past. The light was fading fast, making the scene even more desolate than before. Mahood opened the door and got out. Maybe a bit of exercise would calm his nerves. A thin rain was now blowing across the dreary sedge, and almost immediately he began to feel cold, damp and uncomfortable. But he pulled up the collar of his raincoat and walked slowly to a point closer to the road, where he had a clearer view in both directions.

Almost at once he saw the headlights, little more than a dim glow in the mist, but soon crystallising into two clear points of yellow light. He turned and went back to his car.

The other vehicle was coming on very slowly. Was that just because of the mist, or was the driver looking out for him? The lights grew steadily brighter, and he could hear the car's engine now. It seemed to slow down as it approached the knoll. It was almost at a snail's pace. But then, with a swish of tyres, it slid past the narrow opening where Mahood was parked and continued on its way.

Fifty yards on it stopped. There was a pause, then the car backed up the road, swung into the rutted entrance and parked beside Mahood.

McFaul slid down the window. "Sorry I'm late," he said. "Thought I had a tail back around Stranorlar, so I took a side-road and made sure I lost him."

Mahood nodded. "That's OK. Glad you made it." He lit two cigarettes and handed one to McFaul.

The other shook his head. "You know I don't smoke those things," he said.

Mahood nodded vaguely, and threw the unwanted cigarette into the wet grass.

"You've settled in then?" McFaul asked.

"M-hm. House is fine. A bit bleak, and a bit too close to the village for comfort. But it'll do."

"Met any of the locals yet?"

"M-hm. The local shopkeeper. And the parish priest left a note, but he hasn't called yet."

McFaul drew in his breath. "You thinking of converting?" he said drily.

Mahood did not honour this with a reply, though he knew it was the nearest thing McFaul would get to humour. He finished his cigarette and threw the stub into a nearby puddle.

"Look, why did we have to meet out in this god-forsaken place?" McFaul asked with some irritation. "Isn't there at least a pub we could go to? I'm not a drinking man, I know, but... Or would it have been all that bad to meet in your house?"

"It's best this way. I don't know the pubs well enough yet. It might look suspicious. And I don't want visitors to the house for the moment. I probably seem suspicious enough to the locals as it is. But if I keep having visits from strange men in raincoats..."

"Men in raincoats! You make me sound like some sort of pervert..."

Mahood smiled a slow, wrinkled smile.

"Perhaps you'd prefer one of our female colleagues to come?" said McFaul, just a little sniffily.

Mahood shook his head. "You're the only one I trust."

There was a short silence, before Mahood spoke again. "So tell me the worst," he said. "What did the hearing produce?"

McFaul leaned back in his seat. "Postponed for two months. To gather further evidence, they say. They may want you back for that." Then, after a pause, he said. "Don't worry, you'll be OK. You can count on me to back you up."

Mahood nodded slowly, but said nothing.

"I've heard," said McFaul with a dry laugh, "that Baird wants to give us both a medal. Make us into heroes… But the Chief Constable isn't so sure."

Mahood made a dismissive noise.

"And the… other thing?"

"The sale of the house?" McFaul hesitated. "Catriona says she agrees. But she wants you to come back and clear out… Deirdre's room. In fact… she told me to get the key from your neighbours and go in and… take some things to give to you. I'm sorry, I hope you don't mind…"

Mahood made a vague gesture with his hand. The other man fumbled inside his car and then pushed something like a cardboard folder out of the window and tried to hand it across the gap between the cars. For several moments the folder hung there between them.

"I brought these, some of her things… photographs and the like. And there's a book there too. Catriona told me to bring it. It's called… 'Mountains in Asia'…" McFaul looked across at the other man. "She said it would mean something… it would mean a lot to you."

Mahood turned and looked at the folder. His face was grim.

"Is she trying to be kind, or cruel?" he murmured.

"What was that?" McFaul asked in surprise. But Mahood didn't answer. He simply shook his head and pushed the folder back towards McFaul.

"No, take them away," he said. And for the first time his manner was abrupt. And the deep calm of his voice had wavered, just slightly.

"So what do I do with them?" asked McFaul, perplexed.

"Put them back where you got them from."

McFaul put the folder beside him on the passenger seat and leant back.

"Anything else I can do for you?" he asked in a strained voice.

Mahood shook his head again.

They sat there in silence for another five minutes. McFaul glanced over at the man in the other car. But it was almost dark now, and Mahood had his head bowed, as if lost in thought. McFaul saw the other man's shoulders rise and fall, rise and fall, but there was something oddly uneven about the movement. He looked away.

From out over the sedge came the mournful cry of some water bird, and the faint whisper of the wind in the long grass and heather.

"I'll see you in a couple of weeks then," said McFaul, and turned his ignition key.

4

Shamie waited in an alleyway across the street from Conlon's. Conlon's was the local betting shop, and he knew that was where Donal MacManus usually spent at least part of the afternoon. He had to do it, he just had to ask Donal about his cousin Micky. He had set his mind to it several times, but each time chickened out at the last minute. This time he was determined to go through with it.

Donal had gone in almost an hour ago. At about twenty to three. That meant there was probably a three o'clock race somewhere. The problem was that he would almost certainly stay on for the three-forty-five, and the four thirty as well. And it had started to rain, a thick drizzle, the sort of rain, Shamie knew, that would soak you within a couple of minutes.

He tried to shelter under the projecting eaves of the shop on one side of the alley. But the wind was beginning to gust, and it kept blowing spray round the side of the building, so that within a few minutes he was as wet as he was going to get. In other words soaked to the skin.

He hung on, nevertheless. If he didn't confront Donal this time, and ask him what had happened to Micky, he knew he never would…

Micky had been the great hero of Shamie's boyhood. He was six years older than Shamie, a tall, good-looking fellow much fancied by the girls. But that had never made him big-headed. He had never been above talking to his young cousins, Shamie and Kieran and Liam. He'd always found time to spend with them, down by the harbour, watching the boats, or walking along the cliffs towards the big mountain, talking with them, telling them things, opening their minds to the wide world beyond Killoole.

As he stamped his feet in the alleyway to keep warm, Shamie remembered one particular day many years before. They had gone further than usual along the coast eastwards, and happened on a bleak and rather scary place on the cliff-top overlooking the sea.

On the cliff's edge stood a single row of ruined, two-storeyed buildings.

"That's the old coast-guard station," Micky had told them.

"Why is it all ruined like that, Micky?" Kieran had asked.

"It was burned down a long time ago, Kieran, in the troubles. By our boys."

"What do you mean, our boys?"

"The IRA, who were fighting the British."

"Were the coast-guards British then, Micky?"

"They were in those days, Liam."

"I heard that our Dad's grandfather was a coastguard, Micky."

"Aye, some people had to work for the authorities... to make a living. But there were other members of the family in the IRA."

"I heard that Great-uncle Cormac was in the IRA, Micky," said Shamie. "Is that true?"

"It is true, Shamie. And he was proud of it."

"The IRA are still fighting, aren't they, Micky? Up in the North?"

"They are. I reckon they'll be fighting until the Brits finally pull out and leave Ireland for good."

"If the Brits go, will the Protestants go with them?" asked Liam, who was the youngest in the family, and the most naive. "What do you think, Micky?"

Micky screwed up his face, summoning all the wisdom and experience of his seventeen years.

"A lot of them will go, that's for sure," he said finally. "The Orangemen and people like that. But I'm sure some of them will stay. The good ones. Donal MacManus says there are some good Protestants, and they'll be able to stay. If they accept that we're all one Ireland and all..."

"How would Donal MacManus know?" said Liam scornfully. "Our Mam says he has no brains, because he drank them all away long ago..."

Micky went thoughtful after that. "Donal's a strange one," he said finally. "He lives most of the time up there in the North. Only comes back at Christmas and in the summer… My Dad thinks he's probably in touch with the boys fighting up there, but…"

Micky had never finished that sentence. Shamie saw that he didn't really know what to think about Donal's connections in the North.

That conversation had taken place years before, when Shamie was still quite young. But Micky's hesitation had stuck in his mind. Micky had nevertheless confirmed, on a later occasion, that Donal was some sort of Sinn Feiner, and knew all about the struggle in the North. And that was why, now that Donal was back living in the village, Shamie wanted to talk to him.

He wanted to find out what had happened to Micky. His cousin had left the village several years ago, and never come back. There were rumours that he had gone to the North, to Belfast. Had he got involved in the violence? Had he joined the IRA, maybe?

But if so, why had he never come back?

Had he been killed maybe? Shamie wasn't sure, but he thought somebody would surely have said that if it had been the case.

The rain was getting heavier, and Shamie was now frozen to the core. He had just made up his mind to leave, when Donal's squat figure appeared at the entrance of the bookie's.

Normally Donal went home for an hour or two to rest before he came back down into the village to spend the rest of the evening in Mulligan's bar. Shamie had wanted to waylay him somewhere along the road, away from the main street, out of everybody else's sight. But this time, instead of turning up the curving road towards the Foreland, he shambled off in the other direction, down the street towards the pub. Shamie ran after him.

"Mr. MacManus, Mr. MacManus," he called. "Can I have a word with you?"

Donal had just reached the entrance to the bar. He stopped and turned a surly, flushed face towards the youth.

"What do *you* want?" he growled, none too pleased at the interruption. He had just blown a cool fifty on three successive races and was in a foul mood.

"I wanted to ask you about my cousin Micky, Micky Walsh. You remember him? He hasn't been back home for four years now, and I wondered if you knew what had happened to him..."

MacManus glared down at him, his face growing darker by the second.

"Because, Mr. MacManus, people say you know a lot of things... about things like that." Shamie was conscious of just how lame this sounded.

The rain had turned to a deluge, and water came trickling down from Donal MacManus's close-shaven head on to the coarse wrinkles of his face. They said Donal had been a boxer in his youth, and he still had the build of a light middleweight, slightly gone to seed.

"How should I know?" he answered gruffly. "How would I know anything about it? Ask your father, can't you? Or your uncle... You're Brendan Walsh's cub, aren't you? Well, ask him."

Donal moved into the little porch that led to the bar. He knew the boy couldn't follow. He was under age, and though Mulligan didn't care much about rules and regulations - in the winter the bar often stayed open all night long - he was strict about keeping kids out.

"Please, Mr. MacManus, I did ask him, and all he did was give me a cuff round the back of the head. 'Don't bother yourself with things that don't concern you!' he said. Well that just made me want all the more to know what happened to Micky. So I went to Micky's Da, Uncle Joe. But all he did was give me a queer look and tell me that Micky had gone to England to work, and that's all I needed to know. But there *is* more to know, isn't there, Mr. MacManus? I heard he went to Belfast, and that..."

"Why all this interest so sudden?" asked Donal, turning back towards Shamie, his scowl deepening. The rain was still beating down relentlessly. MacManus took the boy by the shoulder and pulled him in out of the rain. He fixed him with his bloodshot eyes, still gripping the shoulder of the boy's anorak.

"Why all this interest all of a sudden?" he repeated.

Just at that moment the bar door burst open and a red-haired man with a thin, pale face pushed through from the bar itself, rolling a barrel of beer. He glanced at the two of them, standing there streaming wet, and nodded towards the barroom.

"You can take the boy in if you like, Donal. Mulligan's not around today, and the two of you... you look like drowned rats."

Donal's scowl only deepened, but before he could stop the boy, Shamie was in through the door. By the time Donal had followed him, the boy was already perched on a stool in the corner by the open fire. He looked defiantly across at the burly man, demanding some response.

Donal stood there looking angry. He glanced round the room. Fortunately it was empty, save for the boy. That appeared to calm him a bit. He waited for the red-headed barman to pass him and go back behind the bar. Then he went over and sat down near Shamie. Keeping his voice as low as possible he growled:

"I asked you already, why the sudden interest in Micky?"

"It's not sudden. I've been wanting to know for years..."

MacManus suddenly lost his temper, and a second time he grabbed Shamie's lapel. "Who put you up to this? Who told you to come to me and ask questions? Was it your father? By God, if it's that self-righteous..."

He stopped, realising that the barman was staring over at them from behind the bar. It was the new barman, the one they called Pat. He hadn't been there more than a couple of months and Donal didn't know him very well. Lord knows what stories barmen spread about. Word might go round that he, Donal, had been molesting young boys in the bar. Better go easy.

And the boy, he saw, was scared out of his wits.

"No, sir," he was saying. "It wasn't my father, Mr. MacManus. I swear. It's just that I always liked Micky, and no one will tell me where he's gone and why he hasn't come back, and Micky himself it was who said that you used to be... well, that you had friends... in the IRA." The boy said this last bit so softly that Donal MacManus had to strain to hear him. He looked at the boy with a mixture of scorn and disbelief. Then his unshaven chin suddenly twitched, and he let out a low, ironic laugh.

"Is that what he told you?" he said. "Micky Walsh?"

"Yes, Mr. MacManus."

MacManus loosened the grip on his anorak and gazed out the window, towards the rain-soaked street.

"Well, all I have to say to you, young cousin of Micky Walsh, is this. I have no idea where your cousin is, or what happened to him. And that in my opinion your father and uncle are right. Don't you go bothering yourself with things which don't concern you and will only land you in trouble... All right?" And he patted the boy on the shoulder. "Sorry I scared you. Now, hop it!"

"I'm not going till you tell me something!" said Shamie defiantly, his voice rising.

Donal glanced round at the bar again, then turned back to Shamie and leant over him.

"Look, you little piss artist," he hissed, "I'll tell you something about your cousin if you like..." He hesitated, and his manner suddenly became gentler. "But it may not be what you expect... And I can't tell you here..."

"Where then?"

The barman had momentarily disappeared into the back room, and Donal no longer felt the need to whisper.

"You know where I live, in the Back Lane? Come round there some time, in the evening. But make sure no one sees you. All right?"

Shamie realised this was as far as he was going to get that afternoon. He nodded.

Pat had now returned to his post behind the bar, and Donal rose and headed in that direction. Then he turned and looked back at the bedraggled figure of the youth moving towards the door.

"And don't you go round telling people I'm Gerry Adams's best friend," he said loudly, with a false laugh. "If only it were true..."

Shamie trailed out of the bar. The door closed gently behind him. And from inside he heard the low rumble of Donal's voice as he engaged Pat the barman in conversation. Then there came the lighter sound of Pat's reply. For a few minutes Shamie stood in the shelter of the porch, listening to the murmur of voices inside, staring out at the rain as it continued to beat down hard on the surface of the road.

Had he made a breakthrough? When Donal had told him to come round to his house he had felt a sudden burst of hope. So Donal did have something to tell! But the more Shamie thought of it, the more his initial enthusiasm began to wane. Did Donal really know anything, he wondered. Or was he just trying to get Shamie off his back?

Shamie also realised he was just a little scared. Would it be safe to go round to Donal MacManus's house alone? The big man had a fearsome reputation.

5

Father Brian pulled into the car park above the harbour. From here he had a clear view across the rocky inlet to the headland where the grey house stood.

He needed time to think. He was still nervous about going there. He didn't, after all, know who this man was. No one had contacted him from another parish to tell him one of their flock was moving his way. All he knew was that the man was from the North. Maeve Meehan the post-mistress had told him he spoke with a strong northern accent, probably Belfast or somewhere that way.

Perhaps the man was not, after all, one of his parishioners.

It happened. There were Protestants from over the border, professional people mostly, who came and bought holiday homes along the Donegal coast. Not very many round here, admittedly. But further north, the Lough Swilly area and round that way. Understandable. Beautiful country.

Yes, the new owner of the "Bastion" was likely one of them. So it probably wasn't his duty or business to go calling.

But what if the newcomer *was* a Catholic? He wouldn't know unless he called. And it would be a friendly thing to do, anyway, to drop in and introduce himself, whoever the man was and whatever his affiliations.

Father Brian left his car and set off on foot, following the road which curved upward round the narrow inlet. Several times he decided it wasn't worth while, he wouldn't after all call at the big house. He'd just pop in and see Daisy Gallagher in the cottage just beyond. She was over 90 now, and he'd heard she had a bad cough last week. But each time he began to think this way, he went back on his decision, telling himself it would do no harm to call with the new man.

So when he reached the corner where the plain, wrought-iron gate barred the track up to the house he simply went for it, pulling back the bolt and letting himself through. He stood there for a few seconds, half expecting some angry guard dog to come barking down the lane. But the only sound was the low whisper of the wind through the bare branches of the fruitless apple trees. And a moment later his feet were scrunching up the rough driveway towards the forbidding edifice on the brow of the hill.

He pressed the doorbell, but heard nothing inside, no sharp tinny rattle, no melodious chimes, no nothing. He pressed again to make sure he had pushed hard enough. But no, the thing clearly wasn't working. Unnerved, Father Brian was about to leave, but on impulse he turned back, and taking hold of the large metal knocker gave it a firm rap.

The door opened almost at once.

The man holding it ajar was grey, like the house. That was Father Brian's first impression. And well above average height. Must have been a sportsman in his time, the priest thought. A rugby player most likely.

Father Brian stood there, expecting the man to say something. Perhaps just an inquisitive 'Yes?' But he said nothing, and the two of them stood looking at each other for several moments, in awkward silence. It was Father Brian who finally spoke.

"Eh, hello… I'm sorry to disturb you. I'm Father Brian, the local parish priest…"

The man continued to look directly at him.

"So I see," he said finally.

His voice was not exactly unfriendly. There was even a hint of amusement in the man's expression, which unnerved Father Brian even more than if he'd been openly hostile.

"I left a note a few days ago. But then I thought I'd drop by in person and introduce myself, and… welcome you to Killoole."

"Very decent of you," said the man gruffly, and throwing the door wide open, stood back to let him enter. "Come in for a while." There seemed to be an emphasis on the 'while'.

The priest hesitated. He was now sure the man was not a Catholic, or at least hadn't been for quite some time. And yet he found himself stepping over the threshold, into the lofty darkness of the hall. The man led the way across the marble floor to a tall, wood-framed door. This gave on to a kitchen, a bare functional room with rough plaster on the walls and a plain unvarnished table in the centre.

"Take a seat," said the new tenant, plugging in an electric kettle. Father Brian sat down, and took the opportunity to look round. There was nothing at all in the room except what he had seen at first glance: rough walls, plain furniture and newly fitted white cupboards. Nothing else of note except a newspaper on the flat surface beside the kettle. He strained to see which newspaper it was, but only caught the bold-type headline "… OUT FOR THREE MONTHS."

And then the man turned and presented him with a steaming mug of black coffee.

He sat down opposite the priest and without asking agreement or permission lit a cigarette. A moment later he stood up again, fetched sugar from a cupboard and milk from the fridge, and placed them in front of Father Brian.

"Sorry, not used to having guests."

"That's all right," the priest assured him amiably. "We bachelors, you know…"

The man reacted coolly to Father Brian's attempt at levity. He drew on his cigarette and exhaled the smoke sideways, away from the table. "So what can I do for you?" he said.

The man had a deep and melodious voice, one obviously accustomed to commanding attention. His manner was distant and distracted, but not unpleasant. It still held the faintest hint of amusement. And it was very northern.

"Well, you know…," Father Brian began, "it falls to the priest always to call with newcomers to the community, and make them feel welcome…" The man didn't reply, so he went on. "And you'll understand if a place like this always likes to know who it is that has come among them… Are you a single man yourself?"

This time the silence that followed was even louder, more deliberate.

"I am," said the man finally.

"You've no family?"

A slow shake of the head. And the man's eyes slipped past the priest's head towards the window. Father Brian had the impression they had focused on something very far away, out on the grey, bare hillsides that lined the northern horizon.

The priest was beginning to feel really awkward. What right, after all, did he have to ask such personal questions of a stranger, even in the line of duty, even with the best of intentions?

"I'm sorry," he said. "It's none of my business really, is it? I won't ask any more intrusive questions. It was just a way of breaking the ice."

The man brought his eyes back from the distance, and for a second Father Brian thought he was going to smile. "No, go ahead," the man said. "Ask away." And he took a pull of his cigarette.

The priest gave a nervous laugh. "Well, the next question in the interrogation was going to be: where it is you've moved from?"

"Lisburn," said the man quickly, "near Belfast."

"Oh yes… Not a part I know myself. Passed by it on the motorway."

"A lot of people do."

This was terrible, thought the priest. The conversation was dead in its tracks, and he didn't even know the man's name yet.

"By the way," said the stranger suddenly, putting down his cigarette and reaching over to shake the priest's hand, "my name's Brian too. Brian Mahood. But most people just call me Mahood. So there won't be any confusion." And this time the man did smile, a slow, wrinkled smile which seemed to cost him some effort.

"And you're not a Father, of course," said the priest with another laugh.

The smile faded from Mahood's face. He lifted his cigarette again, and took a long, very deliberate pull.

After another pause, Father Brian said: "I take it you're not really one of my flock. You're not a Catholic, are you?"

Mahood shook his head. "Not a huge number of Catholics in Lisburn," he commented, the note of mild amusement returning. "But don't worry. I was glad of your visit. It was very welcome…"

"So you're not one of those…"

"I'm not one of those who can't see the person behind the uniform he wears." He glanced up. "Or beyond the labels people pin on him."

The priest felt his whole body relax. He found himself smiling. "I like that," he said, "the way you phrased it… And yes, I suppose uniforms tend to be a bit intimidating. Often think it would be better to dispose of this thing" (he indicated his dog collar) "when I do my rounds. People take up such artificial poses when a priest is around…"

The other man smiled faintly, tapping the ash off his cigarette. But he made no comment.

"Someone once asked me," Father Brian continued, "'Doesn't it go to your head, being a priest and having all that respect from people? It must be hard to keep humble.' So I said to them: 'Of course not.' But it set me thinking. And now, just before I say the mass, I always repeat to myself: 'Don't let it go to your head! Keep humble!'"

At first Mahood showed no reaction. Then he nodded slightly. His eyes had wandered again out through the window towards the nearby hills. "It's true," he murmured, his face wrinkling into a wry grimace. "Humility and dog collars don't always go hand in hand." He stubbed out his cigarette, then rose abruptly and emptied the ash tray in a bin near the sink.

Then he looked at his wristwatch.

"More coffee?" he asked over his shoulder. "I've a few biscuits in the cupboard as well, if you cared…"

"No, no," said the priest hurriedly. "I've taken up enough of your time." He also rose. "No doubt we'll see something of you in the village, even if you won't be at the parish Bingo on Saturday evenings."

Again the tall, grey man was silent.

"I try to keep to myself," he said at last.

The priest pushed his chair back under the table.

"But you're welcome to come again," Mahood added quickly, "if you're really hard up for company."

Again only the merest hint of sarcasm in his voice.

"One thing I do have is a few bottles of good malt in the other room… And, as I say, I'm not one of those people…"

"…I know, who holds a grudge against a uniform." The priest had hurried to agree, and accept the gesture. But once again he sensed immediately that he had said something wrong. The other man didn't smile or acknowledge the intended humour. He simply pursed his lips, and opened the door into the dim hallway.

They passed through its gloom together. And after a brief goodbye Father Brian heard the front door close behind him with a heavy, definite click.

6

Some hours later it was Donal MacManus who drove his red Peugeot into the car park on the headland. The big house stood out clear and gaunt across the inlet, with the stranger's blue Mondeo parked outside it.

Donal felt lousy. He hadn't had a cigarette for two days, and it was beginning to tell. He was restless and itchy, and felt as if his bones were the wrong shape for his body. To make matters worse he had finished his last bottle of Jameson's the night before, and he couldn't go to Mulligan's.

The two men might be there.

They had been there the last few days, at the same table in the corner. Donal had nodded to them, and one of them, the big one, had grunted back. But Donal was sure the other one, the little weasly one with the grey hair, had made a vague gesture to the first, as if signalling to him to say nothing.

The third day, when they were in the same place, he tried talking to them.

"You guys just visiting these parts?" he said amiably from the bar.

There was a pause, and then the oversize one said: "Ah, we're just here for the fishing,"

"Sea fishing is that?" asked Donal.

The grey-haired man made the same gesture to his companion.

"Aye, sea-fishing…"

"Who are you going out with?"

"What?"

"Who are you going out with? Which of the local boats?"

"Ah, we're not doing it from here," said the man with grey hair. "We've hired a boat a bit along the coast…"

"Where? Castlecharles?"

"No, Donegal town."

Donal put down his whiskey. "You're a long way from base, aren't you?" he said, looking at the men curiously.

The older one nodded to his friend and they rose to their feet. "That's right," he said, with a bland smile. "And we have to be on our way now. Talk to you some other time maybe…" And they left, nodding on the way out to the barman. They had both left their drinks unfinished.

"What do you make of *them*, Pat?" Donal had asked the barman.

"They're from the North," said Pat.

"Well I kind of worked that out myself," said Donal drily. "But do you really think they're here for the fishing?"

Pat shrugged. "They've been in here for the last three days now. Stay about two hours and drink only one, two pints. Then they disappear about the same time each day. It's as if they're waiting for somebody, but he never comes…"

Donal put his drink down and went to the door. He looked out, but the street and its straggling line of houses was totally deserted, except for a mangy black cat slinking round the corner of Conlon's. The two men had vanished in double-quick time.

His first thought was that they were connected with the man in the big house, the man whose name, he had discovered, was Mahood. He was from the North, Donal had heard, and that had immediately put him on his guard. Maybe the two men had a rendezvous with Killoole's new resident at the same time every day, and that's why they left the way they did. But the more he thought about it, the less likely that seemed to be. Something told him that the "Bastion's" tenant and the two 'fishermen' didn't have much in common. He'd seen the man from the big house a couple of times now, and had watched him from a distance. He was tall, clean-cut and middle-class. To Donal he seemed 'educated'. These new ones were more the sort of people Donal was used to mixing with. They had probably gone to school somewhere in the maze of red-brick terraces that made up working-class Belfast, though from exactly where he couldn't work out. Whatever side they came from, they clearly felt ill at ease, out here in the 'Wild West'.

So who were they? Suddenly the old fear was back, after so many years. Had *they* come back to check up on him? It was *they* who had told Donal to go, to leave Belfast and go home. He was slowing down, they said, didn't react the way he used to. He was a liability, they said. It had all seemed too easy, too forgiving, and he had always wondered why it happened as it did. Had someone suspected him, guessed he had made it possible for the young lad to get away? Had someone made accusations? Maybe not everything had been forgiven and forgotten, as they had assured him when he left.

So on the fourth day Donal hadn't gone to Mulligan's. Instead he was sitting here, watching the house on the headland, waiting to see what he could see.

He was prepared for a long wait, but in fact it was mercifully short. He'd been in the car park less than half an hour when the tall man came out. He got into the Mondeo and drove down the lane to the road. When he turned left, up the hill away from the harbour, Donal started his engine and with a slither of tyres sped out of the car park, heading up the road after him.

Almost immediately he found, to his annoyance, that there was another vehicle behind him. An anonymous white van. Donal didn't like having vehicles following him. It was something he'd been sensitive to ever since his Belfast days. And he was annoyed that he hadn't noticed where the van came from. Normally he was quite skilful, or so he thought, at making sure he wasn't followed. He put on a spurt, negotiating the sharp curves up out of the village with squealing tyres.

At the top crossroads, near the chapel, he saw with relief that there was no longer any sign of the white van. He could now concentrate on following the blue Mondeo. He'd caught a glimpse of it as it disappeared across the crossroads. The stranger hadn't taken the coast road, either westwards towards Slieve Trascart or east towards Donegal town. Instead he was heading up what people called the High Road, which led up to a saddle in the mountain ridge above the village and then down to the village of Glendoe on the other side of the peninsula. There weren't many places to turn off this road, so Donal was content to follow a good quarter-mile behind, letting other cars overtake him if they wanted to. To his satisfaction there was still no sign of the white van.

Only when they began the descent towards Glendoe did Donal pull closer to the blue Mondeo, to make sure he didn't lose him at one of the turnings in the village.

They were just outside Glendoe, at a stretch where the road went into some trees, when he realised with a shock that the white van was back, right on his tail. He was furious with himself. That was twice now he'd allowed it to happen. Obviously he had been concentrating too much on the car ahead.

Now he couldn't speed up to lose the van, for fear of getting too close to the car in front.

They reached the junction outside Glendoe and the Mondeo turned right along the main street. Donal expected it to stop at any moment, and held back thirty yards or so, in order not to be taken off guard. The car behind him sounded its horn impatiently. Donal made a vague gesture out of his open window. The white van was still following, just behind the car that had hooted. Donal looked ahead, and saw to his frustration that a cattle lorry had turned out of a parking space and was between him and the blue Ford. He accelerated, and soon caught up with the cattle lorry, but its driver was clearly in no hurry. Donal couldn't see anything beyond it. Now it was his turn to hoot. And this time the driver of the cattle lorry replied with a gesture similar to his own, but leaving no doubt at all what it meant.

There was a fork at the far end of the village and Donal was afraid he wouldn't see which way the blue Mondeo was heading. Clearly its driver didn't intend to stop in Glendoe. But where the heck was he going? It was twelve miles to the next town along the coast, and even more if he took the fork inland...

The lorry turned left along the coast road, and to Donal's relief he caught a clear view of his quarry, heading off along the main road inland, back towards the mountains. Donal made a quick turn to the right without indicating, and the impatient driver behind gave him another blast of his feelings.

As he drove past the small industrial estate on the outskirts of the village Donal glanced in the mirror again, and cursed through his teeth. The white van was still there, though it had dropped back some distance behind.

He glanced forward again and saw that the Mondeo had disappeared round the next corner. He accelerated and swung into the straight stretch of road beyond. To his dismay it was empty! Had the Mondeo had time to reach the next bend? He must have. Donal put his foot down even more, and his little Peugeot shot forward, passing a small pub and a car park on the left. The Half Way Inn, the sign said. It was only when he was past it that Donal realised the man must have pulled in there. He couldn't possibly have reached the end of the straight otherwise.

Donal drove on down the road round the next bend, then did a quick U-turn and went cautiously back towards the pub. Another surprise! No sign of the white van anywhere. Obviously he had been worrying about nothing. The van driver must have turned off into the industrial estate.

He turned into the pub car park and there, sure enough, was the blue Mondeo, parked in a corner under some trees.

Donal parked as close to the Mondeo as he could, got out and sauntered towards the entrance. There was a faint skirl of fiddle music coming from the door, and the pleasant, pungent smell of a turf fire. Donal had been here only once before, a long time ago, and it wasn't likely, he thought, that he'd meet anyone he knew.

As he entered, the barman was in conversation with a large red-faced man seated at a table nearby who was recounting what had happened to his luggage on a recent trip to America. He had got it back two weeks after his return, and they sent him somebody else's case as well. A bright red suitcase which was so heavy it must have held a sack of gold!

The story-teller paused as Donal ordered himself a whiskey. Then Donal turned in the man's direction, mildly curious to find what the strange suitcase had contained. But the red-faced man's story fizzled out at this point. He had decided, after all, not to open it, just send it back to the airport.

"Sure they might have prosecuted me for breach of privacy, or something like that," said the man loudly, and the barman nodded in agreement.

There were several other customers dotted round the bar, and at first Donal couldn't spot the man from the house. Had he perhaps gone through to some back room, with the knowledge of the barman? But no, there he was, partly hidden round a corner behind the end of the bar.

Donal had guessed right! The stranger had a rendezvous. He was already engaged in earnest conversation with a person or persons Donal couldn't yet see. He took his drink and went to sit where he had a better view.

He had expected to see two men with Mahood, but there was only one. Killoole's new resident was not, after all, meeting Donal's acquaintances, the 'fishermen' from Mulligan's. The man he was talking to was a total stranger, a thin, angular man with dirty blond hair.

Across the room Donal couldn't hear their words, but he soon saw that the tall man from the house was becoming very emotional. The other took him by the wrist, clearly trying to calm or comfort him. What was this? Were these two homos from the city, come down to meet in secret? No, he decided. If that were the case they wouldn't just sit talking in a bar. There had to be another explanation. Though what it might be he couldn't for the life of him think.

The only thing he could work out was that the dirty blond one had brought the man from the house bad news.

Donal finished his drink and decided he wasn't going to learn anything from just watching the two men. Yet all the seats nearest the men were occupied. And there was no point, he realised, in going and interrupting them. No, he would play it cool. No need to push his luck this time. He would wait and watch.

He finished his drink. The two men across the bar-room were still locked in earnest conversation. Donal rose and went over to order another drink.

As he approached the bar he glanced out the window to the car park. His stomach lurched and he almost dropped his glass. There, parked under a tree just next his own car, was the white van.

Had he just missed it when he arrived? No, he was sure it hadn't been there. And yet no one had entered the bar while he was in there. The occupants of the van must still be outside, waiting.

He put his glass down on a nearby table and walked to the door. Once out in the car park he walked straight up to the van.

It was empty.

He made a note of its number plate. A Belfast number, as he had expected.

But who had they been following? The man from the house, or himself?

McFaul leaned over the table and gripped Mahood's forearm. It was the sort of gentle gesture you did not expect from McFaul, and Mahood looked up quickly.

"They want to know about the headstone," he said quietly. "Catriona phoned me and said she wants to talk to you about what to put on it. She wants to know if you're coming back."

For a long time Mahood did not answer. Then finally he said:

"Is she back in Belfast?"

"No, she phoned from Scotland."

Another long silence.

"I'm not sure I want to talk to her. I don't think I can. Do you think… do you think you could phone her and tell her to go ahead and put on it whatever she likes? I suspect that as far as she's concerned, anything I might suggest… just wouldn't be right."

McFaul hesitated, and took his hand away. "I think she'd really like to speak to you herself."

Mahood straightened up and looked out of the window. He said nothing. He watched a man he had seen in the bar get into a small red Peugeot and drive off. Why was he in such a hurry, he wondered. A few moments later a white van passed the window and set off in the same direction as the Peugeot, back towards Glendoe.

Finally he pulled a piece of paper from his pocket and quickly scribbled something on it.

"That's what I want them to put on it," he said defiantly.

McFaul looked at the note. It said:

> " *'To Deirdre*
> *Who now lives in an apple wood*
> *on an island*
> *beyond the mountain.'"*

McFaul stared at the words blankly. Then Mahood took the paper back out of his hands and scribbled something else. Mahood had added:

> "*'where the sun falls into the sea.'"*

Mahood got up to leave. He left McFaul to pay.

7

It was a warm, still day, one of those days that surprise you in the West of Ireland with their benevolence and calm. Kathleen Dougherty stood looking out of her kitchen window, over the small back garden with its fuchsia hedge to the long grass of the sloping field beyond, and on down to the lichen-covered rocks of the shoreline and the smooth swell of the cove. The gaily painted boats bobbed and swayed on the undulating surface of the water, their rigging clicking irregularly in the gentle breeze.

A large bumble bee droned busily past the open window, and from the long grass there came a constant hum of insects. A single thrush warbled on the small tree to the right of the garden. Even the tree's stunted frame was celebrating on that particular morning, throwing out a healthy growth of new, bright-green foliage.

Kathleen's mood lightened the more she looked out on the serene picture before her. For days, weeks now she had felt increasingly worn down. Nothing seemed to bring her any joy. There was very little that brought even a mild relief from the never-ending cycle of boredom and anxiety. The dull weariness of her life seemed to be growing ever heavier to bear.

But that particular day it seemed to be in remission. For a while at least.

The whistling of the thrush had stopped, and over the thin hum of the insects came the sound of children's voices. And then a slightly deeper voice, that of a youth in his late teens. Now she saw them, climbing along over the rocks near the old boathouse, Shamie in front as usual, Kieran trailing sulkily in second place, which was also normal, and the others bouncing around behind them, chattering merrily among themselves. All, that is, except her Tony. The small but curiously heavy figure of her only child was some way behind the others, moving slowly and awkwardly among the rocks, in his own little world.

He was twelve now, but he seemed younger. He would always seem younger, she knew, because he would never develop the way they would.

She shook herself, to drive away the shadows that were gathering at the back of her mind. On this day she would not worry about him, she would not regret the way he was, she would not grieve for the lost possibilities of a normal life.

It had been a difficult birth, so difficult indeed that for days afterwards she had lain in a drugged paralysis, unable to move or eat or even think. And she couldn't remember their bringing the baby to see her. She always wondered afterwards if that was it, if her child had been damaged in some way during the birth. But at the time they said nothing. When she finally regained some strength, and the doctor came to speak with her, he assured her that everything was well. She had a fine, healthy boy. She and her husband, Tony Senior, had already decided to call him Anthony. Tony Senior thought it was after him. But in her heart of hearts Kathleen knew she had named him after St. Anthony the hermit, who had lived alone but had nevertheless learned to influence people for the good. And become a great healer.

And at first, indeed, the baby had seemed perfect, her own little treasure, as good a baby as you could have wished for, quiet at nights... quiet in the daytime too, though she did not particularly notice that. When she went to look at him he would always be awake, gurgling gently, looking up at the ceiling, gazing at the frills on the sunshade above him, if she had put him out in the garden on a sunny day. That had been a sunny summer, she remembered, full of days like this one.

Now, as she looked back, she wondered if there had not been some indication in those early days, some dullness in his eyes, some slowness in his responses, some sign of what was to come. If there had been, she hadn't noticed it.

And for his first three years there seemed to be little or nothing wrong. Tony was a quiet child. So what was wrong with that?

Tony Senior had left for Scotland when his son was two-and-a half, to work on the oil rigs. At least, that's what he said. He came back fairly regularly for the first year, though the money that he was able to give her was not as much as she had expected. She had been told there was really good money for working on the rigs. But Tony always explained patiently that a lot of it went on his lodgings, his food, and on one trip he had made to America, to visit the rigs in the Gulf of Mexico. He didn't explain very clearly why he had to make that trip.

And soon his visits became less frequent, the payments into their joint account even more so. By the time Tony junior had reached his eighth birthday, his father's visits had ceased altogether. When she phoned the number where he had been lodging, they told her he had left several months before, and they didn't know where. The woman said she thought he had gone to America. Didn't Kathleen know about that?

It was only when she made enquires that she was told that the number Tony had given her was a Glasgow number, and that if he had been working on oil rigs it was unlikely he would have been living all that time in Glasgow.

With hindsight it had been obvious. Tony Dougherty had never been keen to marry her. He had been the only son of a poor widow, and Kathleen's father, Arthur Brady, had owned a fishing boat. That meant that the Brady family, though not exactly rich, lived quite well for those parts. From the start it was Tony's mother who had pursued and ingratiated herself to Kathleen. Tony himself, a handsome man with a cheerful laugh and a coaxing way about him, had been keener on going to dances in Donegal town than visits to the Brady household. And after they were married, when all the trouble started with the baby, he clearly had no stomach for it all. She had asked him several times to come back, to leave his job, just for a while, to help her with the child. But he had made excuses, told her that the job and the money might not last long, that they might not take him back if once he quit... And so on.

For it was around this same time that it became obvious that Tony junior had other problems apart from his absent father. His quietness no longer seemed quite natural. He had been slow learning to speak. When other children at the village play-school were already gabbling away to their parents, Tony would sit by himself pawing at plastic bricks and then suddenly throwing them round the room in what seemed an attack of frustration. When he did begin to form words he spoke very hesitantly, and with a very strong lisp. The other mothers saw it, and talked among themselves.

To make matters worse Tony was not an attractive child. His hair had begun to grow in an unruly, spiky way, sticking out on all sides. He had a small, turned up nose which seemed always to have a sniff. And his eyesight was not good, so that from an early age he had to wear thick, round glasses through which he squinted suspiciously at people. That cut him off not just from the other children, but from their mothers as well. His lack of response when they smiled at him meant that very soon he was shunned by child and adult alike, and labelled a "queer one" by all and sundry.

And as it became more and more obvious that Tony would grow up without a father, Kathleen felt ever more deeply humiliated.

Not everyone was unkind. Her parents helped, while they were alive, but they had died within a year of each other, when Tony was seven. And some of the neighbours had been sympathetic. No, they had been more than that. Her neighbour Maureen had been saintly, frequently offering to look after young Tony, difficult and unresponsive as he was, in order to give Kathleen a break. And she had four children of her own to mind.

But there were others in Killoole who were not at all of that ilk. Some made little effort to hide their mockery, or their condemnation. Couldn't keep her husband. Always had airs about herself, that one. She was always so superior. Thought she would go to college. Always had the boys running after her. And now she's been punished, with a run-away husband and a half-wit child.

Sometimes she had thought, in her desperation, of going away to look for Tony Senior. To bring him back. Or maybe to stay with him, wherever he was. Yes, to get away, get away from this place which had been so hard on her.

But she never did. She had no money to go travelling. And this after all was her home, a harsh place in many ways, but at least better than some dusty and dangerous city.

Yet she still hoped and prayed for some miracle, some chance event which would change her fortune. Some kind and rich stranger who would come and take her away to a better life.

To cover the windows he would have to buy curtains - thick, black curtains preferably, which would not let in a chink of light. The windows were wide and looked out over the endless void of the ocean. He needed the curtains to shut off the view when it got too much for him, to protect him from the feeling of emptiness which nowadays came only too often. Also, in the evenings, he wanted to feel some sort of protective wall, a barrier between himself and the darkness that surrounded the house, with its multitude of watching memories, the ghosts of his and other people's pasts.

He realised that the locals, the people of the village, might think he was blocking the windows to keep out their prying eyes. He imagined that some of them would think he was trying to hide something, trying to keep the eyes of the curious from discovering some dark and dangerous secret. In reality the curtains were to hide the world from him, not the other way round.

He needed to be alone.

Mahood furnished one room downstairs as a living room, and one room upstairs as a bedroom. And then there was the kitchen, which he kept plain and functional. In the living room he had removed the old, dark wallpaper within the first week. It wasn't just stained and rotten from the damp, it was a dismal maroon colour, with a pattern of ornate blue flowers which some ancient owner had doubtless thought was the height of elegance. He found it funereal and repulsive. Yet when he began re-covering the walls with a pastel green he wasn't sure the effect was so much better. He went on papering regardless, and then started filling the room with what he hoped would be a cheerful clutter of carpets, rugs and sofas, followed by a few armchairs, sideboards and small tables. In one corner a television and near it a stereo. And he cleaned up the old fireplace, so he could have open fires in the winter months.

On the first day the room was habitable he hung up pictures, green and fertile landscapes totally unlike the bare and barren country round his house. Another part of the make-believe, he thought to himself, an attempt to insulate both the room and himself from the reality outside.

In the packing chest from which he retrieved the landscapes he also found photographs. Photographs of people smiling at a camera, in casual family groups or, in one case, in a solid phalanx of uniformed men and women. He began to distribute them round the room. But then he came to two pictures in particular which gave him pause for thought. He sat for several minutes with them in his hands. Then he went round the room again and cleared away all the smiling pictures, shutting them back inside the chest.

Upstairs the bedroom was similar to the living room. Bright wallpaper, a soft bed with a thick duvet, plenty of soft mats and chairs. Plus a portable television in one corner. And lots of books. You could lose yourself easily in books. He would also need thick curtains here, to keep out the morning light and allow him to sleep on after a restless night. Unlike the living room this was on the landward side of the house. Its single window looked back towards the coast road as it wound up out of the village. From this window he had already studied the lie of the land. The house was on a promontory, its only access to the mainland was by a narrow, poorly maintained track several hundred yards long. Where the track met the road there was a gate, a plain farmland gate of welded iron. To the right, the road led down around a narrow inlet, with the shop and the post-office, to the top of the village itself, hidden behind the ridge across the inlet. To the left it continued to wind upwards until it reached the crossroads by the chapel, where it joined the main road, the road heading eastwards, back to civilisation.

It was from this window, on an evening some three weeks after his arrival, that he first took note of a vehicle parked above the house, just before the road curled behind some trees and disappeared from view. He would probably not have noticed it if it had been parked anywhere near a house. But it seemed to be in a small lay-by on the seaward side of the road. And if he was not mistaken the same white van had been in exactly the same spot the evening before. But absent during the day.

There was probably a perfectly innocent explanation, he told himself, but his professional training told him he should at least investigate the vehicle. He waited until it was almost dark, then armed himself with a torch and slipped out of the house. Making sure he was invisible from the upper road, he made his way on foot through the shrivelled orchard. Then cautiously, with the torch switched off, he walked up the road to the spot where he had seen the white van.

When he eventually reached the lay-by, the van had gone.

Tony was in wonderland. His eyes skimmed over the page of secret signs, his secret signs. And then he took his copy-book and his felt-tipped pen, and started carefully to form the characters on the top of a new page.

His father had come home one last time, for Christmas, when he was eight. And he had taken Tony and his mother to Donegal town, to the Yellow Moon Chinese restaurant. Tony hadn't liked the food much, except for the slippery brown things his mother said were Chinese mushrooms. But Tony had been fascinated by the red and purple lacy lanterns hanging over the tables. He had watched as they swayed gently when the waiters walked past. And then he had seen the newspaper…

It was lying on a seat just opposite their table, a newspaper covered in strange and wonderful signs. He had signalled to his father who, laughing, had reached over and taken the paper. An old Chinese man appeared a moment later to ask where his paper was, but when he saw Tony pouring over the front page, his mouth open and his eyes glistening with excitement, the old man laughed and said:

"It is all right. He can keep it. I have read it all anyway…"

And he ruffled the boy's tousled hair and disappeared again.

Tony brought the newspaper back from the restaurant, and ever since it had been his most prized possession. Often when his mother told him to go and play with the other children he stole back secretly to his room to take out the newspaper and look at it. And after a while looking was not enough. Quite by chance that Christmas his mother had given him a large box of coloured crayons. One day, a couple of weeks after the restaurant visit, she came into the kitchen and found him at the table, with a blank sheet of her writing paper in front of him, clutching a deep purple crayon. She moved closer and saw that he was copying out the large characters at the top of the newspaper's front page. With almost painful care he would form each character just as they were in the original, with their curves and squares and lines and dots.

Every so often he would make a mistake. Then he would grab up the paper in frustration, crunch it into a tight ball and throw it in a corner. Finally, however, after fifteen minutes of painstaking effort, he had copied the whole row of big characters at the top of the page. All six of them!

When Kathleen first entered the kitchen she had felt a twinge of annoyance. Why was he wasting his time again with some nonsense? Why was he so reluctant always to go out and play with the other children? She knew the answer only too well, but his shyness in the presence of other children still irritated her. And after watching him form the characters for a couple of minutes, she saw what enjoyment it was giving him. Her mood changed entirely. And when she saw all the crumpled pieces of paper in the corner, Kathleen understood how much effort he had put into the drawing. The fact that it was all without prompting, without encouragement from herself or anyone else, suddenly melted her heart. She felt a new and even stronger bond with her strange, introverted son. Kathleen bent down and caressed his untidy hair, and then planted a big kiss in the middle of it.

A little later, in the front room, he saw that she had been crying.

From that time onward Kathleen made no effort to prevent the copying. It was his own little world of fascination and wonder. Let him have it. At first Tony's copies were large, ill-proportioned and clumsy. But after a while he became so adept at copying the signs that he could do them the same size as they were in the newspaper. She helped him adjust from the crayons to coloured pencils, and then felt tips. Soon he was managing to fit each article in the paper on to one of his own pages. He now recognised a lot of the characters. Some of them occurred over and over again, and when he came across them a little shiver of pleasure would visibly pass through his body. He would wave his hands up and down in excitement and make strange noises… almost as if he were trying to pronounce the words, though there was no way, she reflected, he could possibly know how they were spoken.

Some of the characters became his favourites. His most favourite of all was a very simple one, just a box shape with a line across its middle. It was plain and ordinary, with none of the flowery pretension of many of the others. But he confided with her at one stage that he felt that this one was 'his best friend'.

And he now knew the names of some of the people whose photographs appeared in the newspaper. Or at least he recognised the characters which represented those names. He knew they were names because they came up several times, two or three of the same characters written together.

Tony had already copied the whole newspaper several times over. Kathleen asked him if he wanted her to go back to the Yellow Moon and ask for another newspaper. But to her surprise he pulled a face and began to shake his head. No, he said, this one was the best…

And now, one sunny day in late summer, he was busy drawing his characters at the kitchen table when he thought he heard a step outside. Then there was a heavy tap at the door.

Tony ignored it. His mother did not allow him to open the door when she was out. She had only gone up the road to Maeve's shop, but a rule was a rule, and he had never broken it. The person, he knew, would go away if there was no answer, as they always did. So he went on with his copying.

Then a shadow fell across the window. Tony looked up and there was a man there, staring at him. He had a grey, gloomy face that frightened Tony. The boy gave a sharp cry and ran into his bedroom, leaving his copy book lying on the table.

He jumped on his bed and pulled the eiderdown up round him.

It was the man he had seen in the big house! The Ghost Man. Tony had seen his face clearly that time when he and the others had been crouching in the shed, staring across the wet yard at the brightly lit kitchen window. How had the man found him? One of the others must have told him where Tony lived! Was he coming to punish him?

Tony held his breath, listening intently for any sound from outside. The man had come round the side of the house, so maybe he would try the back door. Had Tony's mother remembered to lock it?

A minute or two later he heard voices outside the front door. To his relief, one was his mother's. And there was a man's voice too, a deep, drawling voice. That must be the grey man, the man Tony had thought was a ghost when he saw him at the big old house.

The voices went on and on talking. Tony was becoming more and more agitated. For one thing he wanted to go and do a wee. And then he wanted, badly, to get back to his copying...

Finally the voices moved into the kitchen. He could now hear what they were saying. Something about money, then a silence. Then the man said something about shapes and colours.

Without warning his mother opened the bedroom door. "Come out here, Tony. It's all right, don't be afraid. There's someone here who wants to ask you something."

The man with the gloomy face was in the kitchen. Tony paused at the door when he saw him. He was one of the biggest men Tony had ever seen. And he was sitting at Tony's place, looking down at the flowery shapes and characters spread out over the table.

Tony had transcribed them, that day as always, in different colours. Here there was a whole page of red signs. On another page the characters were all green. On some pages he had done a line of yellow, which was his favourite colour even though it didn't show up very well on the paper, followed by a line of blue, of black and then orange. And the line he had been working on when he was interrupted had a different colour for each character...

The man looked up as Tony came in.

"Did you do all these?" he said in wonder.

Tony looked away and didn't answer. The man frightened him.

But then he looked up, and the man was still pouring over his writing. He seemed to be showing a real interest, not just the sort of put-on interest which adults normally used when they were trying to be kind to Tony. This man seemed impressed. And he seemed to want to know more.

"Tell me, Tony, do you have any favourite characters? Do you recognise the different ones?"

Tony nodded solemnly.

"Show me. Which are your favourites?"

Tony edged cautiously forward and pointed to the box-shaped character with the line across the middle. Then, more hesitantly, he showed him another, a small box with a long, curling tail.

"You like the simple ones, don't you, Tony?" the man said. "Some of these other ones are really complicated."

"It takes me five minutes or more to do some of them," Tony volunteered.

The man nodded. "I bet it does... Tell me, Tony, are these Chinese letters, or Japanese? I'm really stupid when it comes to things like this..."

"Chinese!" said Tony without hesitation. He was about to tell the man the newspaper had come from a Chinese restaurant, but then he stopped because he thought it might sound stupid.

"You know, Tony," said the man, "you must be the only man in the West of Ireland who can draw Chinese characters. Except, that is, for the Chinese people in the restaurants!"

Kathleen gave a small laugh. Tony wondered if the man had read his mind. Or maybe his mother had told the man about the restaurant.

All this time the man had not smiled once. His face was set in a very serious look. But Tony somehow liked that. Most of the adults he knew smiled at him in an artificial sort of way, and treated him like some kind of moron. This man was different.

And yet... he was sitting in Tony's seat! He was preventing Tony from getting on with his copying. He wanted him to go away. Now.

Again the man seemed to read his thoughts. He stood up abruptly. "Sorry, Tony, I've taken your seat. And I probably scared you looking in the window like that." He turned to Kathleen, who had been looking on all the while with a strange expression on her face, partly tense and uncomfortable, partly nervous and pleased. "So you'll do the curtains for me, Mrs Dougherty?"

She opened her mouth, but said nothing.

"Just name your fee. I'd pay you well..."

"Oh, I'd take thirty, I suppose..."

"Thirty!" he exclaimed.

"I'm sorry, is that too much...?"

"Too much? Look, it's a lot of work. I'll give you at least a hundred pounds..."

She waved her hands in front of her face and laughed.

"No, no, I couldn't possibly take that much... I couldn't possibly..."

"It's not as much as you would get around Belfast... Or as much as the work is worth," he added.

"Well yes..." she said finally. "But *you* would have to choose and buy the material..."

"I have it already," said the man promptly. "Rolls and rolls of it. Far too much, in fact, that I got cheap in a Belfast store. But I need someone... an expert... to make it into curtains."

"For just one room, is this?" she asked apologetically.

"For one big room," he said, "with wide windows. The windows looking out over the sea. So it's quite a job. And then for one little room as well..."

"I'd have to do the work here, at home," she said with sudden emphasis. "That's where I have my machine and all..."

He looked at her solemnly.

"Naturally, that's up to you... But you would have to come up and do measurements, wouldn't you?"

She nodded. "Yes, of course..."

For some moments there was silence. Then the man said: "I'm in most mornings, if you'd like to call... How about tomorrow morning?"

She hesitated. The thought of going up to that grim and desolate house somehow unnerved her. But finally she said: "All right, but it would have to be in the afternoon, after five o'clock. I have things to do until then."

In fact she would be at the chapel most of the afternoon. It was her week to do the cleaning, and take the linen away for washing.

"That would be fine," he said.

Tony, meanwhile, had been looking outside and seen the large blue car parked beyond the wall at the end of their garden. "Is that your car?" he asked the man.

The man nodded. "Yes, that's my car. I'm off to Donegal town now, to do some more shopping..." He hesitated for a moment. "You wouldn't like to come with me, Tony, would you?"

Kathleen stepped in immediately. "No, no... Tony doesn't... I mean, he's not used to going in cars with... people he doesn't know..." She stopped, realising she must have sounded a bit abrupt, and looked awkwardly at the floor in front of her. "I'm sorry, I know that sounds a bit unfriendly, but... well, it's true, Tony hasn't been in a car... or anywhere... without me... for years."

The man looked at her. "All the more reason for him to go out when there's a chance," he said.

There was a pause. Then the man said: "But of course it doesn't have to be today. Maybe both of you could come out some day. The next time I go to Donegal, maybe..."

Kathleen nodded, still looking at the floor. "Yes... that would be nice, some time. But I think Tony would like to go on with his drawing today. Once he's started he doesn't like being interrupted, do you Tony?"

Tony just sat awkwardly, staring down at his sheets of characters.

"Some other day, then..." said the man, turning towards the door.

"Maybe..." Kathleen began, but her voice trailed off.

He looked at her enquiringly.

"Maybe next Saturday," she said finally.

"No, we can't go that day, Mam," said Tony, suddenly agitated. "That's the day of the regatta!"

"Regatta?" asked the man. "They have a regatta here?"

"Oh yes, I'd forgotten. All the villages up the coastline have their regattas. Oh, it's a big day here in the village..."

"Ah, well we can't go to Donegal that day then... I'll probably see you here in the village... I presume it all takes place down by the harbour."

She nodded.

The tall man turned to go.

"I'll be seeing you, Tony! You'll have to teach me some of those Chinese letters some time, OK?"

Tony said nothing. He seemed to have gone back into his shell.

Kathleen closed the door behind the man and came back into the kitchen, lost in thought. She looked down at Tony, who had already re-commenced his slow, painstaking work on the characters.

Normally, she reflected, he was very possessive about his work. He never liked people to see what he was doing, or even know about it. And yet with this man he had opened up, cautiously at first, but with increasing confidence. He had talked, just a little, about his 'signs'. He had tried to share something of the pleasure he got from them.

He had almost treated the man like a friend.

9

Donal struggled along the street and began to climb the twisting road back to his cottage. He was rather the worse for wear. It happened like that now and again. He decided just to have one more, for the road. And then it became another, and so on. Now it was well past midnight and there had been quite a few 'anothers'…

He was also baffled.

The last couple of evenings Little and Large hadn't appeared in the bar. Nor was there any trace of the white van that he assumed was theirs. He scoured the village, walking the whole length of the street, from one car park to the other. He had then climbed up the winding street to the chapel, glancing in all the parking spaces beside the houses. There were a couple of cars with northern registrations, but no white van.

They must have gone. He felt a weight slide off his shoulders.

Maybe they'd gone back to Belfast, or wherever it was they came from. Maybe they weren't after him at all… After all, it was over three years now since he'd left the North. Why should they come for him after such a long time?

Maybe it was, after all, the new man they had come to watch, the man up in the house. If that were the case, there was no reason for Donal to get involved. He'd just be attracting attention to himself.

Yet if they did come back to the bar, Donal decided, he would go up and confront them. Ask them to their faces what it was they wanted. What it was they were really fishing for in Killoole. Because they sure as hell weren't looking for fish, of that he was certain!

He had spent most of the evening on a stool by the bar, swilling his stout round the glass, passing occasional comments to Pat the barman. This was where he felt most comfortable, right at the bar, at the centre of things. Nobody could ignore him here. People came and went, and they were more or less obliged to say something to him, to acknowledge his presence. And as time passed, and the sinister pair made no appearance, the more relaxed he had become. He had convinced himself that the two were no more than a couple of odd-balls who had ventured beyond their normal haunts, possibly out of curiosity. Nothing to worry about at all. As the effect of the beer grew stronger he decided that life was, after all, definitely worth living...

It had been well after nine when the bar door opened with a loud click and the two men walked in.

Donal's heart sank.

It had been raining heavily outside and they shook themselves and stamped on the ground to get rid of the wet from their mackintoshes. They had both been wearing khaki canvas caps when they entered, which they now took off. It was them all right, the grey-haired ratty one with the gloomy face, and the younger, thickset one who looked as if he fancied himself and wanted to pick a fight. Little and Large. Moocher and Macho.

They ordered pints and moved to their favourite table in the corner. He let them settle for a few moments and take a couple of draughts of their beer. Then he ordered a new pint for himself and set off unsteadily towards their table.

"D'ye mind if I join you, gentlemen," he said as affably as he could, though the tension he felt made his voice stony and flat.

They looked at him suspiciously, but said nothing.

"I wondered what sort of fish it was exactly you were angling for in these parts?" he began.

There was no immediate answer, so he ploughed on.

"And by the way, what part of Belfast would you be from?"

The two men looked at each other, which they seemed to do a lot, and just sat there.

"What is it to you?" asked the big one finally. He was giving Donal the hard man stare.

Donal took a long pull from his glass.

"Well, now, I've lived all over the city at one time or another. I was just wondering if you might know a few of my old haunts..."

The weasel-faced one took a sip of his beer and squinted at Donal.

"That's one thing you don't do with people from Belfast," he said in a dry, high-pitched voice. "Ask them what part of the city they come from... It's like... a give-away."

Donal raised his eyebrows. "Oh, really?" he said with feigned surprise. "In what way did you mean?"

The man gave him a cold stare.

"I think you know the way I mean," he said drily.

But Donal had carried on, trying to dig out slowly, bit by bit, what they were about and why they had come, attempting to impress them with his extensive knowledge of "the city". That's what everyone in the North called it, as if there were only one...

But now, three hours and many pints later, Donal was not a whit wiser. And considerably worse for wear. Who were those guys?   At first they had stuck to their monosyllabic, non-committal answers. That convinced him all the more that they were definitely hiding something. But after a while he wasn't so sure. They really didn't seem to know much about anything. Or at least they knew to keep off controversial subjects, like who ran the taxis in a particular area or who was on the rise in the various loyalist or republican political parties. When that topic came up they clammed up altogether. And after little more than half an hour they buggered off altogether, leaving him puzzled and annoyed.

Yet one thing he did find out. It had taken no more than a few minutes to figure out they were not who he had originally thought they were. They knew nothing about the Falls Road or Andersonstown... or at least nothing that suggested they had ever been there. And from his gentle probing, or what he thought was gentle probing, he had rapidly come to the conclusion they were not even from the right side of the road, the right side of the 'peace wall'...

These guys had to be loyalists! Or at least Prods of some description. They had tried not to show it, obviously realising there were not too many of their type in Killoole. But Donal had not been taken in. It was the way they talked about things. The way they averted their eyes and looked away when he made even mildly nationalistic statements.

And his first impression had been right - they really didn't know the first thing about fishing of any sort.

So what were they doing here?

He stumbled on a large stone in the road and almost pitched into the grass that covered the ditch. But he caught himself just in time. He paused for a moment, to clear his head enough to be able to go on...

If they were Prods, then they *must* have something to do with the guy up in the big house? But what? Were they collaborating with him in some way? Or the opposite – were they spying on him? Had he some dark secret, like Donal himself had, that he wanted to hide... and had these two tracked him down?

But that didn't seem to fit the facts very well either. These guys didn't seem to have the wit to track anyone down! There was something very fishy about the whole situation...

What the heck! Perhaps, after all, the two were just anglers, very ignorant 'beginner' anglers, or sightseers of some sort...

Donal struggled on for a while, until he turned the bend and got a view of the headland and the building on it. One solitary light, high on the landward side.

It was a dim light, only a thin crack. Obviously there were heavy curtains pulled across the window. The same room, the same light every evening, as Donal made his way home from Mulligan's. What did the man do up there, the tall man with the grey hair? Donal had seen him in the village several times, once coming out of Maeve Meehan's store, once buying a take-away supper from McConnell's Fish Bar, and once walking alone along the mole out towards the entrance to the harbour. But the man never seemed to want to engage in conversation. When Donal had spoken to him in McConnell's he had simply averted his eyes and walked quickly out with his packet of greasy fish.

That made Donal all the more determined. One way or another he was going to find out who this stranger was, and why he had come here to Killoole.

10

The upper floor of the old house had more light than the ground floor, but if anything it was even more frightening.

Tony stood at the head of the stairs and looked along the cold, empty corridor to the window at the end. It was a strange, gleaming window with a pattern of green and red glass in the middle, and it gave off a glow that filled the corridor with a ghostly light. He was now more than ever certain there were ghosts in this house. And though he was equally sure he would not see any of them (it was daytime, after all, and everyone knew ghosts only came out at night) that was not much consolation. Things that you knew were there, but could not see, were much more frightening than things you were able to see.

He didn't want to move down that corridor, or approach the window. The secret they held couldn't be seen or heard, but he had absolutely no doubt the place did hold a secret, some cold, dark secret that it would be better not to know. And yet he stood there several minutes, transfixed, staring down the corridor at the window and the strange light radiating from it.

He had been heading for the room with the bed, the room where he had found the book. They had visited it earlier with his mother and the man, to take measurements. The man didn't stay long. He showed them the room and the window, and was about to leave when he saw Tony staring at the book that lay on the bed.

It was a large book, with a black cover and brightly coloured pages. Most of these were in varying shades of blues and greens and browns, what he knew were maps. He had always been fascinated by maps. There were several on the walls at the school. But he had never before seen such beautiful ones, with such intricate lines and so much writing. He had great difficulty in reading the names. They weren't the familiar words of the special reading books he worked through with his mother. He could make out individual letters. X was his favourite, and also Z - because they seemed to come so rarely. But there were more of them than usual in this great book of maps. Especially on one page with a large map of a country whose name, he could see, began with a letter C. Though he wasn't totally sure, he guessed that the country was China...

The man had seen him staring at the book and told him he could look through the pages, as long as he was careful not to tear or mark them in any way. He had poured over the book all the time his mother had been taking the measurements for the curtains. And when she had finished, after only ten minutes or so, he asked if he could stay with the book. But she had said no, this was the man's bedroom, he wouldn't want young boys sprawling about on his bed with their dirty feet and hands... Reluctantly he had followed her out of the room and down the stairs...

But now his mother was busy talking with the man in the kitchen, drinking tea and discussing when she would have the curtains made, whether she could come and hang them herself, and so on. Tony had wandered out of the room...

And carefully, quietly he had started to climb the stairs. He wanted to look for the book. He wanted especially to look at the page with the Xs and Zs, and lots of Gs, the page he was convinced was a map of China.

He hadn't reckoned with the eerie red light. He hadn't noticed it earlier, when he was with his mother and the man. But now as he ascended each stair it seemed to grow brighter and brighter. Nor had he reckoned with the scary feeling that seemed to take over his whole body as he came closer to the top. Least of all had he reckoned with what he saw when he reached the top, the glowing window lit from behind by the fading glow of the evening sunlight which bathed the corridor in frightening shades of green and red, trying, it seemed, to attract his attention, lure him towards the window and whisper some awful secret in his ear.

Tony stood transfixed for a moment at the top of the stairs, staring along the corridor in fascination and horror. He was on the point of turning and running down the stairs. But he found he was right beside the bedroom door. He turned the knob and pushed his way into the room as quickly as he could.

He found the book and took it on to the floor. That way he wouldn't put his feet on the bed. And he could read it better as well. He had left the door ajar so he could listen out for the voices of his mother and the man downstairs. Yes, he thought he could still hear them. Or was it the sound of the wind murmuring in the eaves of the house? The wind, he noticed, was getting stronger. They might have another storm that evening, his mother had said as they walked up to the house. And now indeed the faint sighing of the wind round the gables was growing ever louder.

He tried to forget about it and settle down with the book of maps. He found another wonderful page, with another country where the names, this time, had a lot of Ps and Rs and As and Os. He looked at the name at the top of the page and discovered it was an I country, like Ireland.

The door of the room slammed suddenly shut.

He was immediately cut off, alone, isolated. He could no longer hear the voices downstairs. He could hear nothing. Except the wind over the roof.

He lay for a few moments with his book, his nerves suddenly on edge. Strong as the lure of the wonderful map book had been, he now wanted more than anything to leave this dark, enclosed room with its sloping walls and ceiling. He now felt hemmed in, imprisoned.

Carefully, respectfully, he took up the map book and laid it back on the table near the window...

As he did so the lace curtains billowed out in front of him, revealing the gnarled and twisted trees of the orchard beneath the house. The ragged shadow of a cloud, driven by the gathering breeze, slid rapidly over it.

The shadow passed, replaced by a pool of unexpected sunlight. And there on the far side of the field, caught in the sudden brightness, standing alone and looking straight up at him, was the figure of a man. A single, tall man in dark clothes...

Tony turned and ran to the door, but then stopped. What was there out there? Along the corridor, the strange, glowing corridor where he had felt the presence of long-dead people and dark events?

But he had no alternative. He had to escape from the room, past the end of the corridor and down the stairs as quickly as he could.

He grabbed at the handle and twisted it. The door opened and he was in the corridor. He glanced along it. It was empty, but just for a moment the glow through the window faded and darkened. Only to burst out anew, with a new and vivid brightness.

Again it was trying to capture his attention, trying to lure him down the corridor.

It wanted to tell him something.

But he didn't want to stay. He didn't want to know. He fled down the stairs.

He clattered round the sharp corner and plunged towards the darkness of the hall. Several steps above the bottom Tony lost his footing and tumbled head first on to the smooth stone of the hallway floor.

He was in darkness. The first thing he felt was the cold. But miraculously he felt no pain. He picked himself off the floor, and looked up. There were dark looming objects all round him. The great ticking grandfather clock. The enormous mahogany chest of drawers. There was barely any light here. Just a distant red glow high above him and a faint glimmer from the glass of the front door. In panic he looked for the door to the kitchen.

But something made him turn his head in the opposite direction, towards the front door. And there, framed by the clouded glass, was a dark, motionless figure.

Was it inside the door or outside? In the murky light he couldn't make out. But it was definitely the figure of a man.

Tony froze with terror. The man he'd seen across the orchard! How had he got here so soon?

The boy cried out in fear.

Then he turned and ran. Anywhere. Into the dark.

All at once there was bedlam. Tony crashed into something heavy and brittle, and it shattered on the hard floor. There was a loud clatter, as one door burst open, and then another. There was shouting, and Tony was blinded by a sudden surge of light.

He looked up, and found the tall grey man standing over him, anger on his face. And behind him his mother.

"Please mister, I didn't do anything!" pleaded Tony. "Please don't hit me!"

His mother bent down and almost pushed the man away.

"It's all right, Tony, it's all right. Nobody's going to hit you! What happened, my love? What was all that noise?"

He fell into his mother's embrace and burst into tears.

"Please, Mam, I think I saw a ghost," he said.

"There there, Tony, there are no ghosts here. Only me and Mr Mahood!"

"I saw a ghost, over there by the front door."

Mahood strode over to the door and flung it open. A moment or two later he came back. His face was still dark, but seemed to have lost some of its anger.

"What exactly did you see, Tony?" he said in a gentle enough voice, though it shook slightly. "What sort of ghost did you see?"

"I didn't see him right," said Tony, still trembling with fear. "But it was a tall, dark man, over there just inside the door. Or maybe outside…"

"No," said Mahood grimly, "I heard the door slam. I think you're right. He was inside… I must have forgotten to close it when I let you in."

Kathleen was still clutching Tony's head to her bosom.

"I think he's frightened because there are stories about this house," she said, "about it being haunted."

Mahood reached over and patted Tony on the shoulder. "It's all right, Tony. There are no ghosts in this house. I think it was probably somebody who… came to look for me."

Kathleen slowly relaxed her embrace round the boy and they both stood up.

"So where did he go?" she asked.

Mahood didn't answer.

As he and his mother walked down the track towards the road, Tony looked round at the bare grass and rock. "There's nowhere he could have gone, Mam," he said.

She didn't answer, but tightened her grip on his hand.

"Mam, I don't want to go to that house again," said Tony.

Kathleen nodded, and glanced back at the house. Behind it the sky was leaden.

"No, Tony, I don't think I do either," she said.

11

The wind wasn't the same here, he thought. There were no trees for it to torture and shake. There simply were no trees worth talking about. At nights Mahood heard the waves beating on the rocks beneath the house and the wind swirling round the eaves and gables. But that thick rustling, gushing noise of branches heavy with leaves just was not there.

He remembered it from another world. From another time, from another place, where there were green hills and fields and lakes…

And trees, trees everywhere, over gentle lawns and shrubs and flower beds. There was wind, yes, but a different sort of wind, full and rich, not the wild, crabbed wind from the sea that pried and probed round the walls of this gaunt house of his, every day, every night…

He remembered one place and one time in particular…

He had been sitting in his car, in the car park beside a large red-brick building, watching how the wind would periodically surge and lift whole branches of the nearby chestnut trees. It was the height of summer, and the trees were laden with their full adornment of broad, spreading leaves. They rose and fell in the breeze as he watched, in a slow, calm dance of satisfaction and contentment.

Out beyond the great chestnut trees was the parkland, and he could just see a short stretch of the river before it turned in one of its graceful bends and disappeared beyond a grassy hill. And from behind the hill he could see the two arrows pointing upwards, the spires of the rival churches competing for dominance of the skyline.

Why, he was asking himself, had they decided to send their daughter to this school, set here in a small country town so far from where they lived? It had seemed such a good idea at the time, to get her away from the worst of the violence. And he had thought that living with his sister and her husband, who were childless, would bring her "experience" of coping with the wider world. Catriona had always been doubtful about the idea, and now, three years later, he had finally decided she had been right and he had been wrong.

All that he had succeeded in doing was dig an ever widening gulf between himself and his only daughter.

He had been delayed by a case and arrived only after the ceremony began. He opened the car door and got out. Then he slowly walked towards the building and entered.

He followed the distant sound of a female voice and soon came to the main hall. Some worthy lady with grey hair was trying to give life to the spoken word. Her theme was how to make the most of opportunities. Mahood found a seat at the back of the hall and sat down to listen. Or rather not to listen. Instead he searched among the bald pates and brightly coloured hats for the two heads he knew would be there. Finally he found them, the blond and the auburn, hatless and rigid, faced firmly away from him, towards the platform and the lady of experience. Not a hint of movement, of the need to turn and see whether he had arrived, whether he might just this once have fulfilled his promise to be there.

The prize-giving, he found, had already taken place. The speech came afterwards on this particular occasion, so he did not even get to see his daughter receive her one small prize...

Now they were walking back to the car, Deirdre wedged awkwardly between him and her mother. In her hand she clutched the book she had just received. "Mountains of Asia". A curious choice, he had thought at first. But then, after reflection, he decided it was in fact entirely logical. His daughter had a fascination with places, locations. And particularly with mountains. In her three years at the school she had won prizes in one subject alone, Geography. And she had done it again this year.

"So when are you off?" he asked his daughter as the car coasted down the long avenue through the trees back towards the main road.

"Off?" she asked, genuinely puzzled. "Where to?"

"To see your mountains of Asia?" he said, though he knew his attempt at light- heartedness would almost certainly fall flat. To his surprise she smiled.

"Oh, some day, I suppose… Though I'd be afraid I might just be a bit disappointed if I ever did get to the Himalayas…"

"Really?" her mother exclaimed. "If I'd ever had the chance, I know I'd have gone for it, like a shot… an experience like that…"

"Oh you're probably right," said Deirdre. "But the way I look at it is that if you have a book like this, you can get a huge amount of pleasure out of it and… well, you don't actually have to go to those places, do you?"

"Oh, but there's nothing like the real experience!" objected Catriona.

For once Mahood agreed with her.

Deirdre said nothing.

They drove on in silence. When they reached the roundabout outside the town, Mahood asked:

"Where to then?"

Catriona, in the back seat, opened her eyes. "Aren't we going home then?"

"No," he said, "come on, let's celebrate for once." The times when they were together, just the three of them, were not very frequent, and he was conscious just at that moment that he wanted to make the most of this one.

"Well, I suppose we could go to the *Fair View Inn*?" said Catriona.

"We always go to the *Fair View Inn*," said Deirdre with a sigh. "And it's so… well, traditional."

"So where do *you* want to go, Deirdre?" asked her father.

She seemed to think deeply for an endless amount of time.

"Well… there's a new Chinese opened in the town centre. Called the *Lotus Blossom*. Would it be too daring to try there? Or somewhere like it?"

"I don't like Chinese or Indian," said her mother, pulling a face. "I've told you that before…"

But they dined at the *Lotus Blossom* nevertheless, in virtual silence.

Donal checked the float at the end of his line and once again cast out into the clear waters of the harbour. It was a windless, grey day, with just a hint of rain, but he still hoped the afternoon might bring him just a little bit of cheer. Normally he was never happier than down here, near the fishing boats, with nothing more to worry about than the next cast.

That particular day he would have been glad of any sort of calm or reassurance. But it was stubbornly reluctant to come. He sat back in the battered old folding chair that he always brought down with him from the house and gazed across to the mole on the other side of the little harbour. Beyond the rigid line of grey stonework loomed the uneven outline of Slieve Trascart, its lower slopes wreathed in a thick blanket of mist. The mountain's dark, double-headed summit stood out sharply against the steel grey of the sky beyond. For some reason Donal shivered at the sight. Trascart didn't normally have that effect on him. Must be getting old, he said to himself, to let a mountain trouble my day's fishing.

The night before, he had phoned Frankie, his one remaining contact in Belfast following his ignominious departure from the city. He hadn't phoned for over a year, and Frankie didn't sound very friendly.

"What do you want?" had been his first question, direct, challenging, in the rising, querulous tones of the 'big city'.

"Just wanted to know how yez all were over there..."

"We're fine... but why the interest?"

"Ah well, I was just wondering if the brethren are having any regrets about kicking out their star centre-back," he joked.

There was a long silence at the other end of the line. Then Frankie's voice came on again.

"Look, Donal, that's no laughing matter. There were those who thought you got off too light..."

"I know, I know, Frankie, but for Jeez sake, that's why I'm phoning. You were my one real friend at the end..."

"Donal, don't count on it. You know what I'm telling you, brother... don't count on it."

Another silence. It was Donal who broke it.

"Look, are you trying to tell me something, Frankie? Has something happened. If so, just spit it out, friend. Just let me have it straight…"

"No, no, Donal, don't get me wrong. It's just… well, it sounded as if you wanted to get involved again, and that… that would be a bad mistake. Keep well clear, my friend. As I say, there are those who always thought you got off far too light, and that you were… and still are, a bit of a security risk."

"A security risk? What do they mean a security risk…?"

"Donal, Donal, just listen to me. You know yourself that there were two or three guys… and one guy in particular… who was suspicious of young Micky from the start. You know the head case I mean. He always said we didn't know much about Micky, he wasn't from a Republican family, and all that… You heard it yourself, Donal. So when Micky disappeared, and the finger of suspicion was pointed at you…"

"Aye, and pointed by the very guy you're talking about! I know!"

"Yes, well… you get my drift, Donal? Just don't think of coming back, ever. There's those that still have it in for you…"

Donal had lived with those suspicions for four years now. As each year passed he'd begun to feel just a little more secure.

But the call to Frankie had brought back the fear.

He realised, as he began slowly to pull in the reel, that he'd forgotten to ask Frankie about a man called Mahood. Ah well, it would have to wait a week or two now. Frankie obviously didn't like him phoning too often.

12

Shamie stopped at the end of the lane to think. MacManus's cottage was a hundred yards or so off the main road, on an un-tarred track that led up to the old quarry. Shamie had gone that way many times, though he was always glad when he was past the cottage, because it always had a brooding, menacing air about it. Like its owner.

Then he decided he had nothing to lose. After all, he was just going to pass on a bit of information. Then he would turn round and go. And if the information was useful to Mr. MacManus, or anyone else, then so much the better. They would know in future that he, Shamie, was on their side. He could be relied on to run messages, and maybe more than that in the future.

He trudged steadfastly on up the lane until he was in front of the old, discoloured wooden gate. Beyond it was a rough enclosure, unpaved, with a wheelbarrow parked at one side and miscellaneous junk strewn in every corner: an untidy coil of plastic piping, a pile of grit, and under a waterproof sheet some firewood. On the far side of the enclosure, up a set of concrete steps, was the door of the cottage itself, painted an ominous black.

Tentatively he opened the gate and made his way across the yard, glancing furtively up at the two blank windows on either side of the door. Then he was tripping nimbly up the steps. There was a plain white button to one side of the door, and he pressed it.

The door flew open and there was MacManus, in braces and a half unbuttoned shirt. As usual he was unshaven, and even to Shamie, who was used to strange and pungent smells, he stank.

MacManus stared at him blankly, but then his face softened. "Oh, it's you," he said. "What can I do for you this time?"

"Can I come in, Mr. MacManus?"

Donal's eyes narrowed suspiciously, but after a moment he stepped aside and ushered the boy in.

"You're in luck," he said. "I've just made a cup of tea… Or would you maybe like," he chuckled, "something a wee bit stronger?"

"No, no, Mr. MacManus. I've only come to give you some information."

MacManus put the kettle back on the range with a clump. He turned to the boy.

"Now have you forgotten what I told you the last time? I'm not interested in what your uncle or your cousin or Paddy McGinty has told you…"

"But you told me to call round…"

"Aye, I must have been drunk or somethin'… Or maybe I just wanted you to go away and stop badgering me."

"But you said…"

"I said nothing!" Donal slammed the kettle down again. "I told you I know nothing about your cousin… what was his name, Micky?"

Shamie sensed a weakness. Donal was playing too dumb to be real. Clearly he did know something.

"Well anyway," said Shamie casually, "whether or not you're going to tell me anything about Micky… I have something to tell you."

He waited for a response, but when none came he went on. "It's something I think you'll be pretty interested in… I mean that anybody would be interested in." The youth put on a coy expression. "But I think that you, seeing as you know more about these matters than most people, I think you'll be specially interested."

Donal had been pouring tea into two mugs. His eyes narrowed again, and Shamie thought there was going to be another angry rebuttal. But after a moment Donal said:

"Go on then. Sit on that chair and tell me." He handed Shamie one of the mugs.

"You understand… that my source for this information" (Shamie thought the word 'source' sounded good. He had worked out this part of his speech very carefully) "the source for this information is a bit…" (he couldn't think of the word) "isn't a very good one. But the information itself is so interesting that I think you'll agree it's important..."

"Will I indeed?" said Donal, his lip curling back into a faint smile. But he went on looking at the boy steadily, and took a sip from his chipped blue-and-white mug.

"But before I tell you, I want you to promise something in return."

The smile faded from Donal's face.

"And what's that?" he asked flatly.

"If I give you this piece of... important information, will you tell me a bit more... just a bit more, it doesn't need to be everything... about what happened to my cousin Micky?"

Donal set his mug on the table a bit too quickly, and a splash of hot tea fell on the formica surface.

"It's just... Mr. MacManus... like I said before, that no one will tell me anything about him, and he was good to me when I was younger, he was my only good friend. I miss him. I want to know where he is, what's happened to him. I don't even know if he's alive, or whether..."

The boy was on the point of tears. Donal, clearly unused to dealing with emotion, sat back in his chair and looked sideways, and then at the mug, which he had taken up again.

"Well, no, he's not dead... At least, I'm sure he's not. As far as I know he's not."

"So you do know something, Mr. MacManus?"

Donal looked at him slyly.

"I'll make a bargain with you," he said. "If what you have to tell me really *is* interesting..."

"Oh it is, Mr. MacManus..."

"...Then I'll tell you something about your cousin. Though I warn you, it isn't much. And it probably isn't what you're expecting. So have we a deal?"

Shamie considered the offer for a few moments. Then he said:

"The guy in the big house, he's... well what I've heard some people call... a Black Bastard!"

"What! He's from Africa?"

The big man, he saw, wasn't taking him seriously.

"No, no, you know what they mean in the North by 'Black Bastards'..."

Donal wrinkled his forehead and pretended not to understand. "You mean... he's one of those Orangemen who wear Black Sashes instead of Orange?"

Shamie began to lose patience.

"No," he said, scowling. "I mean he's one of them. A policeman... RUC!"

"RUC!" Now Donal was forced to show an interest. "And how do you know this?"

"Because Tony Dougherty told me. You know, the 'little Moron' we call him. The one who's as simple as the moon, as my granny says."

MacManus laughed. "Ha! You mean the little omodon who always rolls his eyes and talks to himself! So you think I'm going to believe something that little half-wit says!"

"But he says he heard Father Brian tell his Mam. And then he heard the man say it himself. When his Mam asked him about it, when he came to call..."

"The man from the house came calling at Kathleen Dougherty's! And her still married...!" He gave an evil chuckle. "The dirty baste!"

"Tony said that the man told his mother not to tell anyone. That he had secrets that people might want to find out. And that he didn't want people prying too much."

MacManus stopped smiling.

"So why are you telling me this?" he asked coolly.

Shamie hesitated. He didn't want to make this large, intimidating man angry. Especially not here, in his own house, where he could do what he liked with you.

"Well, I thought you might like to pass it on to someone… to someone you know who might be interested…"

MacManus put down the mug again. For several seconds the fingers on the mug handle twitched nervously. Then he rose to his feet and bent forward, his powerful frame leaning over the boy.

"Now listen to me, you young eedgit," he said hoarsely. "I want you to leave now, and I don't want ever to see you here again with your stories and your gossip and what you call your information." The man's voice grew louder as he went on. "And I want you to understand this, once and for all. I am not interested in your information and I have nobody to pass it on to! I have nothing to do with anybody you think might want to hear there's an RUC spy in our midst, even if that is what he is! Have you got that? Now, you little fool, get out and don't come anywhere near here again!"

And he pointed dramatically to the door.

Shamie rose quickly and was almost out of the door when he suddenly stopped and turned.

"You, you promised to tell me about my cousin Micky!" he said in a voice quaking with emotion and resolve. "You did. You promised."

MacManus glared at him from under his heavy eyelids, but then his expression changed. A twisted smile took hold of his face.

"Well, so I did. So here's what I have to say about your cousin Micky… When he was eighteen Micky Walsh went away to the 'City', as they call it in the North, because they only have one. He went away to be a student, and while he was there he fell in with a 'bad crowd', terribly wicked people who wanted to change the way things were by using big bad things called armalites…"

"So he did join up with the IRA! I knew it!" said Shamie softly.

"But he didn't join up for long! Because he found after a while that these wicked people wanted to make him do things which he found upsetting. Like actually using an armalite to kill people. So he tried to back out, to run away…"

Shamie stared at him in disbelief.

"And so they killed him?" he whispered. "His own people killed him?"

An angry gleam came into MacManus's eye. Slowly he shook his head. "No," he said. "Nobody killed him. But he did run away. He ran away to England, or maybe even further, and no one has seen him since… Neither his friends in Belfast, nor his own family. You see *that*, my young friend, is why nobody knows where your brave and glorious cousin is. He's a refugee. For life. In some forgotten hole of the universe. And he doesn't dare come home!"

The truth is sometimes worse than the worst you imagined. That, at least, is what Shamie thought afterwards. At the moment of truth he could think of nothing. He simply stood there, stunned, staring at the steaming, half empty blue-and-white mug in the middle of the table.

He looked up at MacManus, who was standing in the centre of the room with his arms folded, looking down at the floor.

"I've one more question, Mr. MacManus."

MacManus looked up at him.

"How do you know all this?" Shamie asked.

MacManus smiled. One of his crooked smiles. "Can you keep a secret? I mean, a real secret, just between you and me?"

Shamie nodded.

"I was one of those terribly wicked people," said MacManus, rolling his eyes. "One of the people who asked him to do things he couldn't stomach. And do you know… and this is also a secret, between you and me… I think he was right. After he left, I couldn't stomach them either."

The mug still stood steaming in the middle of the table.

"Did you help him escape, Mr. MacManus?"

MacManus, maybe out of an old habit, moved quietly to the window and glanced outside, as if someone in that lonely place might have been eavesdropping.

"I think you'd better be going now, my lad," he said. "We've swapped enough information for one day."

He opened the door, and again he looked out into the grey daylight, as if to check that no one was watching. Shamie was still reluctant to leave.

"Do *they* think you helped him, Mr. MacManus?"

MacManus gave him a friendly box round the ear. "There are always people who have no faith in their fellow men," he laughed. "Let them think what they like! They couldn't prove anything, then or now."

As Shamie trudged back down the lane, he wondered if people like that really needed proof.

13

The regatta was not quite what Mahood had expected. He had imagined yachts with white sails floating calmly round a bay. But the Killoole regatta, like the others held all along that coast, took place in and around the confines of the village harbour. Outside the mole there were rowing-boat races, with teams from all the little ports within thirty miles or so, six or eight men and women pulling on their oars like mad while the crowd on the harbour wall screamed encouragement. And inside the rough rectangle of the harbour there were games: people balancing on a greasy horizontal pole and biffing each other with pillows until one of them fell off into the water; people trying to crawl out to the end of the self-same poles to retrieve a flag; junior rowing races; and so on.

For once the cliff-lined mountain to the West was in sunshine, though the air was so misty that its angular outline seemed almost to shimmer in the air. From time to time a sharper ray of sunlight would settle on some patch of heather or glint on a tumbling watercourse. But for the most part the pale and murky haze made the mountain look even more remote than usual.

On one side of the harbour, outside the fish market, was a small funfair, with shooting booths, rides for the children and roundabouts playing merry, jangling music. And one horrific machine which raised its strapped-in victims high in the air, and then started to roll and shake them about as if they were cocktails in a mixer.

'Do people really pay money to have that done to them?' thought Mahood as he wandered through the crowd. 'Don't they have enough thrills in their lives?'

Then he saw Tony, over to one side, near an ice-cream stall. The boy, with his snub nose and hedgehog hair, was looking on wistfully as a group of girls bought themselves various choc ices and lollies.

"What's wrong, Tony," shouted one of the girls mockingly, "don't you have any money?" And she and the others jostled each other and giggled as they made off through the throng with their purchases.

Mahood moved towards the stall, and his eyes met Tony's.

"Could I buy this young lad an ice-cream?" he asked the red-headed man who was serving.

The ice-cream man gave him a curious look. But then he relented. "Sure you can," he said cheerfully, glancing in Tony's direction. "Looks as if he needs cheering up."

Tony seemed doubtful about the whole thing, and at one point Mahood thought he was going to turn and disappear into the crowd. But when the man held out a cone with a large stick of chocolate protruding from it, he came forward slowly and took it.

At that moment his mother appeared.

"Tony, who bought you the ice cream?" she asked, with a note of reproach. Tony, carefully licking the drips from round the side of his cone, nodded slowly in the direction of Mahood.

Kathleen had apparently not noticed his presence.

"Oh," she said, taken aback. "Thank you... but... but it wasn't necessary."

"All the other kids were treating themselves, so I thought Tony wouldn't take it amiss."

She stood there awkwardly, not knowing what to say.

"Would you like one yourself?" he asked.

"No, no... I mean, I never..."

"It's a great event you have here. Not what I expected at all... Do so many people come every year?"

"Oh yes... more sometimes. But they get a bigger crowd at Bunduff. And Castlecharles is the biggest regatta of all. It's not so far along the coast and a lot of holiday-makers go there."

"Oh well, you're as well not getting all the townspeople."

She nodded. The conversation seemed to peter out after that. Tony had already drifted off, and his mother was about to follow when a burly figure emerged from the crowd and made his way directly towards them. Mahood was not sure whether or not he'd seen this man in the village before. There was something familiar about his shaven head, his bull neck and his hunched, slightly suspicious stance. But that might have been because Mahood had seen many such figures in his time.

"Hello there, Kathleen," said the newcomer. "I saw young Tony there, happy as larry, walking away with his ice-cream. He seems to be coming on fine…"

Kathleen dropped her head non-committally. "We get by, Donal, we get by. But it isn't easy sometimes…"

Donal kept glancing vaguely in Mahood's direction, as if waiting for an introduction. But neither Kathleen nor Mahood offered one, so Donal took one muscular hand out of his pocket and stretched it in Mahood's direction.

"Donal MacManus," he said, examining Mahood's face carefully.

Mahood took the proffered hand. He was about to introduce himself, as he usually did, simply as 'Mahood'. But then he thought twice and said simply: "My name's Brian."

The other man looked at him keenly, as if waiting for more. But when none came he said:

"You the man from the big house?"

Mahood nodded. Everybody seemed to know who he was, even though they'd never actually met him.

"What's it like to live in? A bit draughty, maybe?"

"Oh, I've papered over the cracks and done up a couple of rooms to make them comfortable…"

"He has, Donal," put in Kathleen. "Mr Mahood asked me to do him some good thick curtains, to make his sitting-room nice and cosy…"

She stopped, and with a characteristic gesture looked down at the ground in front of her. Donal had switched his gaze from Mahood to her.

"Is that right?" he said.

Mahood suddenly felt he was no longer needed here.

"OK, Mrs Dougherty," he said, "thanks again for the curtains. And let me know how you get on with the application?"

"Application?" Donal pricked up his ears. "What application would that be?"

"For the special school in Sligo," said Kathleen hurriedly. "I've applied for Tony to go there. They say they can do wonders with the kids nowadays…"

"Oh I'm sure they can, Kathleen," said Donal.

Mahood nodded in his direction and moved away from the ice-cream stall.

"So you've been up to the big house yourself, Kathleen?" said Donal amiably enough, though there was a new, steelier note in his voice.

"Yeah," she said, tossing back her head. "He wanted these real thick curtains made, from cloth he'd brought down with him, from Belfast… or wherever it is he used to live. Maeve put him on to me."

"So what does he do up there all the time?"

She shrugged. "He's not up there all the time. I think he goes out a lot… At least, that's the impression I get. It's just a sort of pad for him, you know…"

"And what has brought him to these parts, can you tell me that?"

"I've no idea," she said with a note of defiance, as if she wouldn't have told him even if she knew.

"I can't buy you an ice-cream can I Kathleen?" he asked, exchanging a sly grin with the ice-cream seller, whom he recognised as Pat, the barman from Mulligan's.

"No thanks, Donal," she said, "I have to be off. Find Tony and get a good place to watch the boats…"

"There's just one thing I wanted to ask you, Kathleen," Donal said as she turned to go.

She paused. "And what's that, Donal?"

"Did you know he was an RUC man?"

She looked at him as if she hadn't heard him correctly.

"Who told you that?"

Donal took the cone the ice-cream seller had just made for him and took a first lick.

"I heard it from a little bird who said *he*'d heard it from your Tony."

The sun was behind her and he couldn't see the expression on her face. She said nothing, just turned round and walked away quickly into the crowd.

Donal turned to the red-haired barman turned ice-cream vendor.

"You have to warn people sometimes about the company they keep," he said.

14

The day of the regatta ended with a great wind. It swooped in suddenly from the Atlantic, carried by a dark bank of lowering cloud. The stalls began to quiver and the tents that housed the betting booths began to pull at their mooring ropes. Litter began to swirl across the quayside and people were soon hurrying for shelter, back to their cars or to the warmth and shelter of Noonan's cafe or Mulligan's bar. The rowing races had already ended and the organisers brought a halt to the remaining yachting events. The stall-owners began to pack up.

Mahood was one of the last to leave, and as he unlocked his car in the upper car park the first heavy drops started to fall. By the time he reached his grey home on the hill it was pouring. He let himself in through the front door and for a while stood there in the dark hallway, as if he had suddenly lost all motivation or sense of direction...

Finally he went into the kitchen and made himself a cup of coffee.

The nights, he reflected, were the worst time. He had underestimated how noisy an old house like this could be, especially on the wild nights when there was nothing to check the fury of the Atlantic gale. It wasn't only the sounds outside, the roar of the waves on the rocks beneath and the wild whooping of the wind as it swept past the gables. No, there were other sounds as well, inside the house, low moans in doorways and creaks up in the rafters, and the rattle of the panes in his bedroom window.

He took his coffee into the darkened sitting room. The new curtains, long and heavy, had been drawn shut since the night before, and he made no move to open them now. He sat in the dark and listened to the rain beating savagely against the windows facing the sea...

These were the times when thoughts and ideas and memories came crowding back, and there was no way to stop them. Memories, for the most part, of violence and fear and horror.

But also, occasionally, of better times... Of conversations, for instance, with his daughter.

His daughter at various ages…

Wasn't it curious how at different ages children seemed to be totally different beings! You never noticed a point of change, a transformation, a threshold. There was no moment, no day or week in which the chrysalis threw off its coat and became the butterfly. But the small, quiet girl of three, with large, sad eyes had somehow become the noisy and boisterous five-year-old, constantly asking questions…

What holds the aeroplane up in the air?

Why is blue different from red?

Why does rain fall down and not up?

Where does the wind come from?

Questions which were sometimes very difficult to answer. Indeed some of them had no answer. Yet such questions, he thought, were prompted by the very impulses that made life worth living: curiosity, fascination, wonder. Delight in the things we didn't understand, but which we knew were beautiful. Life's mystery. Its poetry…

Impulses, he felt in his gloomier moments, which went some way to holding back the slow, relentless decline towards apathy, emptiness and death.

What is the country like beyond the sky? she had once asked.

'What makes you think there is one, Deirdre?' he had replied.

'I don't know… I just feel there is. Or lots of countries… yes, I think there are lots of countries, all the countries that you find in story books.'

'Well then, you've answered your own question, haven't you?'

'No, but I want to know what *you* think those countries are like…'

He had hesitated, his hand poised by the light-switch. He had wanted to say he didn't believe in those countries, but something stopped him. 'I think those are countries where only children live,' he said finally.

She had looked up at him from her bed. 'No,' she said very definitely. 'You will be there too. I'll make sure of that.'

…When she was six, she had spoken to him for the first time of Applewood Island. At this age she was already an angular, awkward girl with long legs, a pale face and abundant, untidy red curls.

"When I grow up," she told him, "I want to travel across the sea. I want to travel *far* across the sea, to visit all the lands there are on the other side."

"*All* the lands?" her father asked lazily. He had just finished reading her a bedtime story, after a long and harrowing day's work. "You want to visit *all* the lands over the sea?"

"Yes," she said emphatically. "And specially I want to visit Applewood Island."

He opened his eyes and looked at her. Slowly a smile came to his face. "Where's that?" he asked.

"Over the sea," she said. "Out beyond the horizon!"

"And how will you get there?" he asked, the smile on his face broadening.

"By ship, of course. They don't have any aeroplanes in Applewood Island."

"Why's that?"

"Because there's no room for them to land! The whole island is covered in apple trees!"

"What, even the mountains?"

"No, you silly man. There aren't any trees on mountains! But you can't land an aeroplane on them either."

He gave way to her impeccable logic.

"And who lives on this wonderful island?"

"Why wonderful *people* of course!" She laughed.

He laughed too. "Why are they wonderful?"

She thought for a few moments, and then said: "Because they are all so different. None of them are the same. Each one of them is completely different from all the others…"

He nodded, a serious look on his face. "Mm, that makes sense... A bit like the rest of us. I mean, people in general..."

"Yes," she went on, not listening to him, "some of them have blue faces and some have green faces. And some have long, pointy ears and some have round, fat ears..." She laughed at the thought of the different types of ear. "Some live in little round houses and some live in the ground, in holes under the apple trees..."

"And are they all happy?" her father asked, struggling to keep his eyes open.

She screwed up her face, in a serious effort to find an accurate answer. "Well," she said, "most of the time, I think... Of course, they have to be unhappy some of the time."

"Why's that?"

"But that's obvious... If you were happy all of the time it wouldn't be any fun being happy! There wouldn't be anything special about it!"

He thought about that one, and looked at her seriously.

"You have a lot of deep thoughts in that little head of yours, don't you!"

She shook her head. "They're not deep thoughts," she said. "They're quite simple really. Very ordinary in fact..."

He smiled again, and turned out the light.

It was a year or two later they first saw the mountain. They had rented a bungalow on the west coast near a long, fine beach which stretched for miles and miles, where the beautiful, curling breakers came tumbling ceaselessly on to the firm yellow sand.

Deirdre had been in raptures. For the first three days, while the weather held, they had played together for hours and hours, she and her father, building sandcastles, dashing into the sea up to their thighs (it was too cold to go any further), blocking the little stream that flowed out from the sand-hills, then breaking the dams to see the huge flow of water burst out over the shining flat sand.

Deirdre's mother, meanwhile, sat quietly under her sun umbrella near the dunes, smiling vaguely in their direction but never joining in. Instead she would read a book or just loll back on her towel.

On the evening of the fourth day, the weather still had not broken. They sat in silence on the veranda of the bungalow and watched the red circle of the sun descend slowly towards the horizon. Before it reached the sea it slid behind the dark silhouette of the mountain on the other side of the bay. It was a rugged black shadow of a mountain which they had been told was called Slieve Trascart. Deirdre said quietly: "I want to go and find where the sun goes into the sea."

Her parents had looked at each other, perplexed.

"What do you mean, dear?" her mother asked.

"I want to find where the sun goes into the ocean. We never see it because it's hidden by that mountain."

"But the sun doesn't go into the sea just in one place," her mother tried to explain. "It goes into the sea... in a lot of different places."

The girl looked at her mother with patient scorn.

"But here... in this place, it goes into the sea behind that mountain. We've just watched it."

Sure enough, her father thought, from that particular spot the sun did set every evening in the same place, behind the same mountain. They had looked out at the mountain every day, from the beach. And what a mountain it was. It always seemed to have a strange, moody air about it, like a wild animal crouching at the ready, waiting to pounce on some unsuspecting prey. And though he had never been there, he had been told that it was a spectacular mountain, falling away steeply on the ocean side in a series of rugged high cliffs.

"We'll go there one evening... tomorrow evening maybe, and take a look."

His daughter turned her head up towards him, her eyes sparkling with pleasure.

"Can we, really? Can we go tomorrow?"

"If the weather's good… What do you think we'll see there, Deirdre? What's it like, this place where the sun goes into the sea?"

His wife looked at him reproachfully. Why encourage her nonsense? she seemed to be saying. But the girl gave the question serious thought, then said:

"I think it's a great wide bay… a bit like this one, only even brighter and sunnier, and with very green grass and very yellow sand… And I think there's probably an island there, on the other side of the bay, which is very difficult to get to. But once you get there, it's got everything you've always wanted…"

Her father looked at her. "Is this the island covered in apple trees?"

She nodded. "Yes, I think so," she said.

"Yes, definitely," she said a moment or two later.

"And I suppose only children live there," sighed her mother.

"No," her husband had said, because he knew better. "Old people can live there too, can't they Deirdre?"

The girl smiled at him in a knowing way. He had remembered. "Yes they can," she confirmed, "if they like. In fact, it wouldn't be much fun with only children… Children can be nasty sometimes."

But the next day the weather had turned. When they woke, a chill drizzle was blowing in off the Atlantic. Deirdre stared out in dismay.

"We won't be able to see the mountain and the island, and the place where the sun goes," she said softly.

"Let's go anyway," her father had answered, trying to console her, "and see what there is to see. There are some huge cliffs there, where the mountain falls right into the sea. And beneath it a fishing port, with lots of little boats…"

Deirdre was not interested in boats, but the idea of a mountain falling into the sea caught her imagination.

"Why does it fall into the sea?" she asked. "And if it keeps on falling, will it not get smaller?"

"In fact it only falls very slowly," her mother explained. "One stone at a time…"

This explanation puzzled the little girl. But her father thought, well at least Catriona is trying, even if the image of stones falling one by one wasn't very compelling. For him the idea of enormous cliffs tumbling into the wild sea was simply exciting. And he knew that when they got there and saw it, the child would understand perfectly why he had called it a Falling Mountain.

But they never did get to the mountain. Either that day, or ever.

The guidebook said there was a fine view of Slieve Trascart from a lay-by, just before the turn-off to a village called Killoole. Mahood had pulled into it, hoping to see at least some of the cliffs. But apart from the grey roofs of the village itself, and the small chapel up to its right barely visible through the rain and mist, there was nothing at all to see.

"Where is the mountain?" Deirdre had demanded. "You said we would go and look for the mountain!"

"It's hidden by the rain," he had explained patiently. "On another day you'd be able to see it from here…"

"We could still go there, and see what's on the other side…"

They were all three silent for a while. Then Catriona said:

"There isn't much point, Deirdre, is there? The sun's not going to come out today. So we wouldn't be able to see where it disappears to…"

"We'll go down and look at the fishing boats," said her father, trying to lessen her disappointment. "There's supposed to be a little harbour in the village."

But Deirdre wasn't interested in boats.

"Come on, Brian," Catriona had said, "Let's go and get something hot to eat. I presume they do have hot food in this place somewhere…"

He nodded.

Deirdre, however, refused to get back in the car. She stayed standing in the heavy drizzle, gazing over the roofs of the village, hoping no doubt that by some miracle the mountain would suddenly loom out of the mist.

"We'll come back another day, Deirdre," he told her gently, "and then you'll see the Falling Mountain…"

To his relief she looked up at him and smiled a strange smile.

"Yes. We'll come here another day. You and me, Daddy. Definitely."

15

Things in the village had gone very quiet.

The waves swelled and sank listlessly on the smooth, algae-covered stones ten feet or so beneath his feet. The water in the harbour seemed for the moment to have lost touch with that limitless store of energy which kept it always in motion, forever fighting against the shoreline. On a day like today, in early September, when the anger and fury of winter tempests were still only a vague threat in people's minds, the warm and lazy air of summer lingered on over the small fishing port. The water's surface lay smooth and greasy, reluctant, it seemed, to throw up even the smallest ripple or break the reflection of the roofs and chimneys on the other side of the harbour.

It had become so still indeed that Mahood, sitting with his feet over the edge of the quay, began to make out on the water's glassy surface the reflection of the distant mountain that hung above the rooftops. Though its smooth contours were misty and pale in the late afternoon sun, its inverted image was quite clearly visible on the gently stirring waters midway between where he was sitting and the steep stone wall opposite.

Slowly he became aware there was someone watching him. He turned sharply, but at first didn't see anyone. The flat expanse between the quay and the higher, outside wall of the mole was deserted. It was only when a quiet voice came from the top of the wall itself that he looked up and saw who it was.

"Are you waiting for someone?" the voice repeated.

"No, no," he said hurriedly. "Who would I be waiting for?"

Kathleen stepped a little gingerly down the stone stairs from the parapet. She always had that slightly tentative air, he thought, as if she was half expecting the ground to slip away from in front of her. And yet, as he watched, he decided her movements were more careful than fearful. They were deliberate rather than timid. As if experience had shown her that you have to prepare each step forward in life before committing yourself to it.

"Well, I didn't want to disturb you in case you were deep in thought," she said, walking up to him. She was smiling. "Some people, you know, prefer to be left to their own thoughts. And... it was so unusual a place to see you sitting. That's why I thought you might have arranged to meet someone."

He shook his head slowly, and turned back towards the harbour. "No, I come here sometimes. It's a sort of natural end to a walk from my house. To the harbour and back. There's no obvious endpoint for a walk beyond the village."

She nodded. "I know what you mean... though you could, maybe, walk to where the upper road comes down to the coast and meets the road from the village. Then you could go back along the upper road and back down to your house."

He pulled a face. "Too long for me. And there's too much traffic on the roads, and no footpath."

"That's true." She sat down on the edge of the quay a few yards away from him. "I mind about ten years ago poor Artie Lamerock got knocked over along that road. At night, it was, and some drunken eedgit came roaring round the bend and didn't see him..."

They watched in silence for several minutes as the water gently swelled and ebbed beneath them.

"A strange place to meet your end," Mahood said finally. "A nothing sort of place. A road going nowhere..."

She glanced at him, screwing her eyes up against the sun, which was now slipping towards the western horizon. "Oh, you mean Artie," she said with a little laugh. "I thought for a moment you were talking..."

She stopped.

"What, about myself?"

"No, no," she said, shaking her head in confusion. "I just... I just misunderstood. It sounded as if it was meant to apply to... well, maybe some of the rest of us."

He smiled. And then he nodded. "Yes, well maybe it was."

She was still embarrassed. "It just sounded, well, so gloomy and... despondent."

He looked across at her. "Hey... what big words we're using today!"

She blushed and looked away.

"Don't worry," he assured her. "That phrase... about the road to nowhere. It wasn't really supposed to have any very deep meaning. It was just one of those things you say..."

She pursed her lips. "All the same, it sounded very... well, just a bit depressing, I suppose."

He didn't reply. They sat there for about five minutes or more, saying nothing.

"Did you think again about an excursion in the car?" he said finally.

She glanced at him sharply.

"You mean...?"

"I mean would Tony like to go in the car to, well, Donegal or some place like that?"

She didn't answer for a moment. Then she said:

"Well, not to Donegal. For some reason he doesn't like the place. I think..."

But she didn't finish the sentence. What she had been going to say was that she thought it reminded Tony of his Dad, and their trips there together. But there were some things you just didn't talk about with strangers.

"Well maybe, up to the mountain? You know, Slieve Trascart... I've heard it's beautiful up there. Really spectacular."

"Oh but would that be safe? I mean, for Tony...?"

"Oh safe enough, they say. If you keep to the track."

She nodded. "I'll think about it," she said. "If it were a fine day."

"Oh it would have to be a fine day all right."

She scrambled to her feet.

"Have to go and do some shopping. For old Norah Quinn. She fell and broke her hip last week and, well, she's probably going to be housebound from now on."

He nodded approvingly.

"Are you going to come round and see Tony this weekend?" she asked. "Saturdays are the best day, because a lot of the other kids go off and do something with their families, so there's no wee gang to hang out with."

"OK," he said nonchalantly. "If I'm invited."

"You're always invited," she said. "You know that." And she turned and strode off rapidly towards the harbour-master's office at the base of the pier.

16

"I'll be coming back to get you in a couple of weeks, Tony," said Aunt Philomena. That's what his mother had told him to call the tall, thin woman who had come all the way from Sligo. And had made it clear, to Kathleen at least, what an imposition that was.

"We'll look after the little fellow all right, Mrs. Dougherty, don't you worry. And he'll fit in with the others, no problem. Won't you, Tony?"

The question was phrased in a friendly way, but to Tony it seemed to carry some sort of threat.

Tony just didn't want to go. He was frightened by the prospect of a big, unknown town. And he was thinking about the man.

He had wanted to ask his mother if the man could come to Sligo some time, to see him. But he'd decided she would only be angry with him if he did. She now seemed to be angry more often than at any time since, well, since his Dad had gone away. When he began to say something about the man, she would turn on him and snap: "Would you stop calling him 'the man'! His name's Mr Mahood. Try to remember that... But for pity's sake don't keep calling him 'the man'!"

But Tony couldn't make himself think of him as anything but 'the man'. The name his mother mentioned just didn't seem to fit.

Tony and his mother followed Aunt Philomena out the front door and up through the small garden to the front gate. A large black van was waiting to take her back to Sligo.

"So we'll see you in a few weeks, Tony," said the woman called Philomena. She got into the van and waved down at them, with a fixed smile which Tony didn't like.

Kathleen waved back, and encouraged Tony to do likewise. But all he did was make a vague gesture with his hand.

He just didn't want to go to the 'special school', however exciting his mother said it would be.

Tony went back to his copying. He didn't know if Shamie's gang was going out today and he didn't really care.

He'd somehow lost interest in the gang in the last month or two, the constant teasing, the endless walks to nowhere along the coast. He preferred spending time with the man.

When he looked back on it, he hadn't really liked the man at first. At least, not in the way his mother seemed to think he did. He had always felt a bit intimidated by the man's large frame, his big hands. And there were other things Tony didn't like too - like the smell of cigarettes he had about him, and that other, sickly smell he sometimes detected, especially in the evening. Tony knew that was from drinking something called whiskey, which his mother didn't like. And then there were his long silences, when he didn't speak to you at all, even when you were speaking to him. Like when they were making the matchstick house together. He would just go on doing what he was doing with his big, clumsy fingers, putting glue on a matchstick or placing it with painful and deliberate care into its place on the roof or one of the walls. He hadn't liked the man when he was quiet like that. Tony had felt a bit angry with him, but also frightened.

And at first the man had also seemed to expect something from him, to be coaxing something from him in a way other people didn't, except maybe his mother. And Tony hadn't liked that. He was used to being left to his own ways and devices. At the beginning he had only talked to the man because the man had talked to him first.

But after a while Tony got used to the man smelling of cigarettes and whiskey. His initial resentment of the man's intrusion into his private world faded. He even began to look forward to the man's visits. When other people came to the house, they didn't talk to *him*. They talked to his mother as if he wasn't there. They talked *about* him, never *to* him. The man, on the other hand, always talked first to Tony. Tony was always included - him and his pictures. Tony liked to think of the carefully drawn Chinese characters as his pictures.

And Tony began to notice that his mother, who was so often unhappy and listless, would somehow wake up when the man began asking him questions. She took an interest in what the questions were, and sometimes even joined in with some of her own. She seemed pleased, and somehow more hopeful, when the man spoke to him. And she was even more pleased when he, Tony, said something in return. His mother would stand there in the background, looking at her son with a strange look in her eyes. As if she were seeing him, the real him, for the first time.

But the most important day had surely been when the man started drawing the signs with him. That day, as Tony watched the big, awkward hand trying to form the difficult curves and dashes with his fountain pen, something tremendous happened. The man was no longer just there beside him, showing an interest in what he was doing. That day Tony felt the man had actually entered his own world and become a part of it. He had begun to share what Tony's life, his strange, isolated but often happy life, was really like. The man with the deep voice had become a friend.

"Don't you ever wonder, Tony," the man said one day, "how the signs are pronounced?"

Tony looked at him as if he hadn't understood the question. In fact he had, but he didn't know what to answer. The truth was that he was so happy in simply copying the signs that he wasn't at all sure he wanted to go beyond that, into the bigger adventure of actually learning what sounds might go with the characters. He was afraid it would be too much for him. That he wouldn't be able to do it. That he would get frustrated and then... and then maybe the whole magic of writing the letters would go, vanish, disappear as mysteriously as it had come. And he didn't want to risk that.

So he simply turned back to his copying and didn't answer the man's question.

"Each one of the signs means something, you know," the man probed. "Maybe some day we could start to learn what they are. And then after that, some day, maybe a long time from now, we could learn how to pronounce them as well..."

Tony shook his head.

The man was looking at him with his strange, misty grey eyes. "We could do it together. You and me... And maybe your Mam, if she wanted to..."

Tony shook his head with all the ferocity he could muster. Then suddenly slammed the palms of his hands on the paper in front of him.

They sat in silence for several minutes. The man went on quietly copying the character he had been occupied with, a complicated one with little horns at the top and broad, flowing strokes opening out like a tree further down. When he had finished it, he showed it, as he always did, to Tony.

"Of course, we don't *have to* learn the sounds, or the meanings, Tony," he said quietly. "If we're happy just drawing the signs, that's fine by me. But if ever the urge takes you to try a sound or two, we could do it together, just the two of us…"

Tony had been staring at the wall, where his mother had hung some of his favourite characters, and the ones she liked too.

"Maybe," he said suddenly, in a remarkably clear voice which took Mahood by surprise. "Maybe we could, a long time from now."

17

It was only at the last minute that Kathleen decided to go with them to the mountain. The previous day she had made up her mind that when Mahood called she would tell him to take Tony by himself. She would tell him she had things to do in the village and would stay at home.

But then she realised that if she didn't go, Tony would hardly agree to go either. He really wasn't used to going anywhere with strangers. And though this man, Kathleen was convinced, really did mean well, Tony would still act up funny at the idea of going without her.

Of course, if anyone saw them going off, her and Tony going off with 'the man from the house', the tongues were bound to wag. So what was new! And when she thought of it, why should she take heed of them? If there was gossip she could take a perverse pleasure in letting it develop, and then go on to prove it was nothing more than just that, malicious gossip.

What finally made up her mind was, strangely enough, Tony's own hesitation. When the big blue car drew up at the front door, Tony himself began to have doubts. He wanted to stay at home, he said, and do his writing.

"But you've wanted to go in the man's car all week, Tony," she told him.

Tony just squirmed and said nothing.

"Well I'm going," she said on a sudden impulse. "So are you going to stay here by yourself all day?"

When they reached the car, Mahood seemed to sense there had been some problem.

"You can come in the front seat beside me," he said to Tony. "Your mother won't mind, I'm sure. And we could stop at the tea-shop on the mountain for an ice-cream..." He knew it would probably be closed, but he didn't say so.

Tony had finally agreed to get into the car, though in the rear seat beside his mother. They set off.

"What is it like on the mountain, Mam?"Tony asked in a whisper as the car climbed up towards the chapel and the crossroads above the village. His voice was small and timid.

"Don't worry, Tony" Mahood reassured him. "There's nothing to be frightened of. Just lots of heather and gorse and a great view over the sea when you get to the top."

"Up there it will be like a new world for you, Tony," Kathleen joined in. "The only thing is, there are big cliffs, and you mustn't go too near the edge."

"He'll be fine. Won't you, Tony? And the weather's going to be good as well."

Kathleen squinted doubtfully at the sky, which was bright but hazy, and said nothing.

They had to take the road along the coast, west of the village. It climbed away from the sea, so they had a fine view out over the coast, down on to the rippled surface of the water. Not too much wind, and broken cloud. Not bad at all, thought Mahood. There was rain forecast, but not until late afternoon.

Soon they turned a corner and were confronted by the great mass of the mountain rearing up before them. A patchwork of pale green fields and rough stone walls, and then, further up, a broad expanse of rougher land, with ferns and heather. To the right the land sloped upward to the long ridge which formed the backbone of the mountain. To the left, separated from the main ridge by a narrow valley, was the great shoulder of the mountain which he knew hid the lowering, ominous cliffs that you could see from Killoole. Their path would lead up the valley between the two spurs, to a point where it came out on the cliff top. Then, all being well, they would follow the track along the top of the cliffs, to get a view of the last great precipices, where the mountain jutted out in a final gesture of defiance into the turbulent waters of the North Atlantic.

The road curled its way up the valley towards a small whitewashed house in a hollow which at the height of the season served teas. There was a car park there, but as Mahood had guessed the tea-house was closed. At this point the tarred road ended. Only a simple track continued, winding on up the valley between the ridges. Mahood knew from the map that it went on for about mile, to a higher car park, quite close to the cliff top. He eased his car slowly past the whitewashed tea house and up the rutted track.

Tony was gazing out of the car window at the wild, rush-covered fields and broken-down walls. From time to time he would let out a small exclamation, and whisper something loudly to his mother.

"There are so many sheep, Mam. Who looks after them all?"

"The farmers, Tony, that own the land."

"But do they stay out at night? Even in the winter?"

Mahood smiled to himself. The lad really was an innocent. There was so much that was new to him.

As they approached the upper car park, Mahood saw there was another car already there. It was a small maroon car which turned out to have a northern number plate. County Down, he noted, as he eased his car past it to the upper end of the car park, near the beginning of the cliff path. So they would not be totally alone on their walk.

There was a plain wooden signpost just above where he parked which said simply: "To the Cliffs". Mahood opened the car boot, took out the rucksack with the food and water, and locked the car.

They set off. At first the track wound its way up through rough fields divided by the ubiquitous stone walls of West Donegal. Then they crossed a style and were in open heath and moor. Up here the breeze had freshened, and it tugged gently at the tussocks of grass and heather as they continued their way upwards. Neither Kathleen nor Tony had spoken since they left the car. Mahood was comfortable with that, and he hoped they were too.

At last they reached the crest of the ridge. The ground suddenly fell away before them and the sea appeared in all its endless grandeur, stretching out to the horizon. A shimmering path of dazzling light lay across its surface towards the hazy disc of the sun high in the western sky.

And below them, where the mountain literally did fall into the sea, the sight was breathtaking. They were on the rim of a huge amphitheatre of cliffs. The precipice began just a couple of hundred feet beneath. The steep grassy slope suddenly stopped, and there was nothing between that point and the sea. They had a clear view of the cliffs to the right, and saw how the grass ended abruptly to give way to an almost vertical drop - rock and screes careering downwards in a dizzying jumble to the restless, gleaming carpet of the water.

The sea was so far beneath them that it looked misleadingly calm and still. Mahood could make out only the merest hint of waves breaking against the bottom of the gigantic cliffs. He knew it was probably not nearly so settled as it seemed.

He looked down at Tony. The boy had screwed up his nose and was gazing at the spectacular vista before them with some awe. Kathleen was standing close behind him, holding his shoulders, gazing down at the great gulf beneath. Her face too betrayed a mixture of fascination and horror.

"Some view, isn't it, Tony?" said Mahood. It was the first thing any of them had said since they left the car. Tony made no reply. Like his mother he seemed transfixed by the view of tumbling cliffs and distant water.

"Let's go on," said Kathleen finally.

"OK," said Mahood. "Tony, just stay with me and your mother, and stick to the path."

The path rose sharply towards one of the high points on the cliff-top ridge. Every so often they would stop in order to take in the stunning views of the cliffs to their left. Mahood kept an anxious eye on both Tony and Kathleen, to check that both of them were happy to continue. So far the path was well away from the actual edge of the precipice. To their right the ground sloped up towards the summit of Slieve Trascart. Mahood noted with just a touch of concern that the top of the mountain was obscured by a thin layer of cloud. The sunshine was now not nearly as bright as it had been.

After fifteen minutes negotiating the rising path, Mahood turned to look back at the way they had come. He could see clearly the point where they had come out on the cliff-top, and beyond it the heather slopes they had climbed to reach it. Then, below that again, were the walled fields and the car park, and away in the distance the winding road up from the little whitewashed cafe.

He noticed there was another vehicle winding its way slowly up the road to the upper car park. It looked like some sort of minibus. Or possibly a delivery van, though Mahood wondered what there would be to deliver up in this remote spot. Perhaps it was a small bus bringing up some hikers.

He turned and they continued along the path.

Now it began to descend quite steeply, and after a few minutes they found themselves at the very edge of a sheer drop into the abyss. The path was little more than a broad ledge cut across a section of cliff. Although there was a rather rickety iron fence along the edge, Kathleen glanced a little anxiously at Tony.

"You all right, Tony? You're not nervous or anything?"

Tony shook his head. But the boy did seem disturbed by the awesome void which was so close to them, and the frightening dark cliffs which they could see on either side. Mahood could feel the boy's tension, as well as his mother's. He told them to wait and went a little way ahead by himself. To his relief he found that after twenty yards or so the path climbed steeply away from the precipice and continued over a grassy stretch some way from the cliff's edge. He went back across the ledge and gently took Tony's hand.

"It's OK, Tony. This bit only lasts a few yards."

As they crossed the fenced section Kathleen took a firm hold on Tony's other hand.

They climbed the grassy slope and found they were now climbing towards the last and highest point on the ridge. When they reached it, they stopped. From here, looking back, you had a much clearer view of the bowl of grey cliffs than they had had from the first viewpoint, on the other side of the amphitheatre. And in the other direction you could see straight out over the Atlantic, looking towards the western horizon.

On that side the land sloped away from them in a long, crooked promontory, with magnificent cliffs on either side. Beyond the final headland was a rocky island.

As they watched, the sun broke through the cloud and turned the sea into a shining, sparkling carpet of silver.

Why, Mahood wondered, did this scene remind him of something? One of those feelings of *deja vu*, no doubt. Odd how it happened so often, the feeling you had been somewhere, experienced something, even in places you knew you had never been before.

Mahood was a few feet from the others, a little behind them. He looked at the mother, her arm resting gently on her son's shoulder. He saw the pale, fine skin, its whiteness accentuated by the wisps of red-brown hair that blew around it. How could such a good-looking woman, he wondered, have given birth to such a graceless child?

His gaze switched to Tony. How was the boy reacting to the view in front of him? Tony, however, was just standing there impassively, gazing out at the ocean, his face screwed up in the pale sunlight. Mahood could read nothing at all in the boy's expression.

What, he wondered, was going through that small and confused head?

Then Mahood suddenly knew why he felt he knew this place. Maybe in a sense he *had* been there before.

This, surely, was the place at the end of the world where the sun descended into the sea? Where the land ended in a bay, and there was an island.

Would there be an orchard on that island out there beyond the bay?

He didn't think so.

Mahood wasn't quite sure what it was he felt in those minutes they spent on the summit. A strange mixture of sadness and elation. He felt he had reached a point where a life that was past and lost merged with another, which was new and open to change.

But also fragile and threatened.

They went on looking towards the West for some time, at the sea churning restlessly round the rocks on the last jagged finger of land before the endless ocean.

Kathleen glanced at Mahood. He was standing there, still as a rock, the wind pulling at the strands of his greying hair. She was aware of a new mood in him, one she was unable to read. She wondered what it was he was looking at so fixedly. Strange that his attention seemed so glued to that desolate headland, and the island beyond. She had forgotten to ask him if he had been here on the mountain before. Did the place perhaps hold for him some long forgotten memory? She didn't ask. It was best, she decided, to leave him to himself.

The sun disappeared again, and suddenly it felt quite chill on the open mountainside. Mahood turned abruptly and opened the rucksack, handing Kathleen some of the sandwiches he had prepared. She saw he was frowning, and when she looked again towards the West, she thought she guessed why. The sky in that direction was rapidly growing darker.

"Let's eat these as we go back," he said. "The weather looks as if it's changing. It may not be much, but it won't be so pleasant up here if it does turn to rain."

Kathleen nodded. It had begun as a warm enough day, but there was now a chill in the brisk wind. And the sky to the West had become so black that it might well be more than just a rain shower.

Mahood handed another sandwich to Tony. The boy looked up at him and smiled.

That, Kathleen thought, was the first clear acknowledgement of Mahood's presence her son had given that morning.

They had brought waterproofs, and they put these on before they started back. As they trudged back along the ridge Mahood handed out more food - plastic bottles of fizzy drink and a couple of bananas. He noted with approval that Tony carefully handed back the banana skin and the paper in which the sandwiches had been wrapped. The boy had been well brought up.

The wind was rising now, and there came the first heavy drops of rain. They had almost reached the place where the path plunged down to the edge of the precipice.

They clambered down the broken rock towards the exposed ledge. In spite of the rough iron railing between them and the abyss it was an extremely scary place. You could really feel the breeze here, tugging at your clothes. And the sea below had been transformed. Its surface was dark and flecked with foam. They could hear, above the mounting noise of the wind, the distant roar of the water beating against the great cliffs.

The rain had started in earnest now, as they slipped and slithered across the rocky ledge along the precipice… Mahood kept close to Tony, urging him to keep well away from the edge. He was very conscious of Kathleen right beside him. At one point he felt her touch his shoulder…

And then, to Mahood's immense relief, they were back on the grassy track again, climbing away from the ledge. The cloud had now moved in to surround them, and when he glanced downwards he could no longer make out the sea. There were only fleeting glimpses of the water far below, quite angry now as the wind whipped up crests of foam and drove long lines of waves relentlessly towards the shore.

They ploughed on for what seemed like ages. And even though they were on the look-out for the turn-off to the car park, they almost missed it. It was Tony who spotted the fragile wooden signpost, shaking in the wind, that pointed to a gap between two clumps of heather.

"Well done, Tony," said Mahood, patting him on the shoulder. "Thank goodness one of us remembered where the path was."

And once they had got off the ridge and were sheltered from the wind it was much easier going. Mahood flicked back the hood of his anorak and felt himself relax as they trundled along together down the slope. Kathleen was striding step in step beside him, and Tony leaping gleefully from tuft to tuft of the bog grass.

He suddenly felt a deep satisfaction. Something he hadn't felt for months, maybe years. He hadn't communicated much with them that afternoon, he thought, but the lad and his mother did seem to have got something out of the day.

They were only five minutes from the car park when Mahood remembered the other car which had been parked there when they arrived. Why had they not seen its occupants anywhere on the mountain?

It was at this point that they heard a man's warning cry. And then the first shot.

18

Mahood ducked automatically, then fell flat on the sodden grass.

Tony, a little ahead of them, had stopped. He had obviously heard the shot too, and turned enquiringly back towards his mother. But Kathleen was just standing there, transfixed.

"Get down, get down quick, both of you!" Mahood urged them. Hesitantly Kathleen lowered herself on to the ground and lay there, looking pale and shocked. A moment later Tony followed her example.

"Keep your heads down!" Mahood called. "Don't look up, whatever you do."

Then there came two more shots. And a sudden volley broke out. At least two people shooting, Mahood thought. Maybe even three. One with a pistol. The others with rifles by the sound of things.

What he could not work out was whether he and his little flock had been a target. If there were two people shooting at each other, then probably not. But in that case who were these people and why had they come here, of all places, to shoot at each other?

There was a sudden lull in the shooting. Mahood heard his own heavy breathing, blotting out the noise of the wind in the surrounding heather. Luckily they were in a small depression. They should be OK as long as nobody with a gun actually stumbled upon them by chance. He saw Tony lift his head to look around. Urgently he called: "Tony, keep your head down. And keep still until all the shooting has stopped."

Then the firing began again, with increased ferocity. Volley upon volley. And once again it stopped abruptly. Was it his imagination, or had he heard, above the scything noise of the wind, the voice of a man crying out? In anger or in pain?

There were several more shots, but they were sporadic now, and seemed a little further away. Then Mahood heard quite distinctly the sound of a vehicle door sliding shut and an engine starting up. Someone was leaving.

Should he go and scout out what was happening? There were no more shots, and he had distinctly heard the muffled sound of the vehicle driving off in low gear. The gun battle, it seemed, was definitely over. But some instinct held him back. If one side in the shooting had fled the scene, what about the other one?

"Kathleen, Tony, keep as still as you can," he whispered. "I'm just going to move forward a little to see what I can see. But you stay here! Whatever you do, don't move until I come back."

Mahood crawled slowly through the soaking grass, keeping as much as he could behind the flimsy shelter of the clumps of heather. The rain was pelting down by now, and the mist had also drawn in. He was soon out of their hollow, creeping towards a low line which he knew was the first of the stone walls.

Suddenly he froze as a figure appeared on his left out of the mist.

At first it was no more than a dim shadow in the rain, but as it advanced towards him Mahood saw that it was a single man, with the hood of his anorak hiding his face.

And in his right hand he appeared to be holding a pistol.

The figure stopped. It was clearly looking for something, for somebody. Probably me, thought Mahood.

The figure was now walking straight towards him. Mahood reached instinctively for the place where he used to wear a holster. But there was nothing there. He did still have a pistol, but on that particular day, a day of innocence and relaxation, he had left it back at the house.

The figure stopped again, just a few yards from him, and tensed. Slowly it raised the weapon and turned it in Mahood's direction.

"Whoever you are," Mahood spoke out, struggling to keep his voice calm, "don't shoot. I have a woman and a boy with me. And I'm unarmed..."

The gunman lowered his weapon and visibly relaxed.

"For God's sake," he said, "why didn't you call out when you saw me?" It was McFaul.

"What in Heaven's name are *you* doing here?" cried Mahood, jumping to his feet. "Here was me thinking you were some IRA hit squad!"

McFaul looked back towards the car park. "IRA? No, these are the other lot..."

Mahood looked in the same direction.

"You mean... Are you sure they've gone?"

McFaul nodded. "I got at least one of them. Maybe hit both..."

Mahood looked at the weapon in McFaul's hands. "With that?" he asked incredulously, nodding towards the pistol.

"Ah," said McFaul with mock modesty, "but I had the advantage. They didn't know I was here..."

"So it was you fired that first shot?"

"No, they fired at me... after I shouted to them to drop their weapons. They were down there, hidden in the heather above the car park. Obviously waiting to pick you off..."

"So how did you spot them?"

McFaul looked at him as if he were an idiot.

"I was here first, of course... We've been tracking these two for some time. HQ got a tip-off from the local guard, name of Flanagan. And you mentioned this little jaunt the other day. Thought I'd take some precautions."

Mahood grimaced. "Once again I owe you," he said quietly.

"You do," said McFaul.

At that moment Kathleen and Tony came hurrying up through the heather.

"Who was that man?" asked Kathleen as they drove back along the twisting road towards Killoole. She was sitting beside Mahood in the front seat. Tony was by himself in the back.

McFaul had stayed up at the car park, to 'tidy things up' as he had put it.

"He said he was a policeman," said Mahood as nonchalantly as he could. He had told McFaul to pretend they didn't know each other. "He said he'd been tracking these two suspects from the North, and followed them up here. But they caught sight of him and opened fire."

None of it sounded convincing, he knew. But it was the best he could think up at short notice. He didn't want Kathleen to know he had been the men's target.

"So it had nothing to do with you?" she said, looking at him pointedly.

He glanced over at her, then turned his eyes back to the road.

"Nothing at all, according to our friend back there."

Her disbelief was palpable. "Who's he working for then?" she demanded. "The *Gardai* or your people, the RUC? He spoke with a northern accent."

"I think he's probably RUC, cooperating with the Guards."

He hated himself for telling her so many lies. And they weren't even very plausible lies.

"Is that possible? Would the Guards allow that?"

He tried to sound convincing. "It has happened in the past… And I've never met this guy, so maybe he's with the *Gardai* and comes from East Donegal. The accent over there is very northern."

She made no more comment, but her suspicions clearly remained. Mahood saw her glance back at her son.

"How's Tony?" he asked. "He's very quiet."

"He's asleep," she said. Her voice was strained and hollow.

As they drove into Killoole, Mahood felt as low as he had felt since he came to the village. Not only had he started lying to the person who had probably helped him most, but he now realised that he had been putting her and her son in danger by inviting them on this excursion.

And he also realised that McFaul had been concealing from him something of which he had been blissfully unaware: that his cover, here in the village, was blown. At least one set of enemies had discovered him, and if it hadn't been for McFaul's vigilance…

How soon would it be before they, or others like them, were back?

19

He could see two people beyond the clouded glass. Mahood shot back the bolt and opened the door. Two men in uniform. One a priest, and the other a rather portly, middle-aged Garda.

"Er, could we come in for a moment, Mr Mahood?" said Father Brian. "Constable Flanagan has some questions he wants to ask you."

The visitors refused the offer of tea. In the sitting-room Constable Flanagan sat stiffly in an armchair and took out the obligatory notebook.

"I have some questions concerning the morning of the 15th," he said unsmilingly. "Do you remember where you were that morning, Mr... er... Mahood?"

"The 15th? That was last Wednesday... Yes, I was up on Slieve Trascart, with Kathleen Dougherty and her lad Tony..."

"It was just the three of you?"

"Of course..."

The officer looked at him coldly. "The lad's teacher, Miss McGinn, has reported he was very disturbed at school, the day after..."

Mahood raised his eyebrows. "Disturbed? In what way?"

The policeman did not answer for some moments. "Disturbed. Upset. What other word do you want?"

Mahood sat forward in his chair. "Look, are you trying to suggest something here? If so, exactly what is it?"

"I would just like to know, Mr Mahood, what exactly happened up there on the mountain that particular day..."

There was a hostile note in the Guard's voice and Mahood found his temper rising. But he forced himself to keep calm. "Look, you're not implying there was anything... improper in my taking Mrs Dougherty and her son for a trip...?"

"No, Mr Mahood," Father Brian interrupted him, "there's no suggestion at all of impropriety. Nothing like that. It's... well in a way more serious than that."

"More serious?"

"If you'll just be patient, Mr Mahood," said Constable Flanagan. "The boy told his teacher that there was some... what he called banging up there. It sounded as if that meant there was shooting..."

Mahood threw up his head and gave a small laugh.

"Yes, that's what I thought at the time... There were a number of sharp noises like shots."

"And?"

The policeman and the priest had their eyes fixed on him.

"Well, I don't know what it was... but it turned out to be a false alarm. Maybe it was just the sound of the wind... it was quite stormy up there. Or maybe someone was shooting... at rabbits or something?"

Constable Flanagan continued to look at him fixedly. "Mr Mahood," he said quietly, "I believe you are yourself a police officer..."

"Was. I resigned three months ago."

"It would have been good for everyone... you know, courteous and that... if you had let me know. Just so that I was aware of the situation, and any potential... shall we say, consequences? But never mind that... If you are a policeman, then you will know the difference between gunshots and... 'the sound of the wind'."

"Not necessarily... I sometimes think I hear gunshots in the middle of the night, and then decide it's just my imagination." He stretched in his chair. "To be honest, one of the reasons I resigned was that the violence was, well, getting to me... Making me imagine things that weren't there."

Flanagan looked down at his notes. "Yes, Father Brian has explained to me that you left the RUC because of... stress. But the boy said they sounded like shots to him. Bangs from a gun, he said. And he hasn't gone through the same traumas that you have..."

"He's quite an imaginative little soul, though... as Father Brian will agree."

The constable pursed his lips. "So did he imagine the other man?"

Mahood raised his eyebrows. "Oh, you mean the man we met near the car park?"

Flanagan nodded, with just a hint of irony.

"He was a man from Co Down... I saw the number plate of his car. He'd been walking on the cliffs too. And he also thought he heard the shots. Stopped and asked if I thought it was safe to go back to the car park..."

"So he knew you were a policeman?"

Mahood gave him a quizzical look.

"No... why? I didn't imply that at all."

Constable Flanagan rubbed his smooth-shaven jaw thoughtfully. Mahood prayed he would not ask about McFaul's gun. He couldn't remember whether or not McFaul had hidden it before Tony arrived on the scene.

Flanagan tried another tack. "So you don't have the impression," he asked, "that this man had been involved in the shooting?"

"No, definitely not. As I say, we decided there hadn't really been any... shooting."

"Did you get this man's address, by any chance? Or his name?"

Mahood shook his head. "Sorry. Didn't think it was that important."

Flanagan gave him another cold stare. After a few moments he asked:

"Do the names McVittie and Thornton mean anything to you?"

Mahood frowned, then shook his head. "I know a few McVitties, but no Thorntons that I can remember... Why?"

Flanagan heaved uncomfortably in the low armchair. "We found them in a van half way between here and the border. Badly shot up. McVittie died last night. Thornton's in intensive care."

Mahood looked at him blankly. "Why are you telling me all this?"

"They were both from Belfast… They were shot with a pistol…"
The Guard suddenly leaned forward. "We've established they were both members of an illegal organisation… So why do you *think* we're telling you!" Clearly Flanagan, for his part, was also finding it difficult to keep his temper.

Mahood saw he needed to calm things. "Look," he said, also leaning forward, "I'm sorry if I seem a bit unhelpful, but one reason I came down here was to get away from this sort of thing. I really haven't come across anyone called McVittie or Thornton, not professionally anyway… I presume by their names that they're loyalists?"

The Guard nodded. "That's what we were told by your people in Belfast. UDF or UVA or one of those…"

Mahood thought again. "I've made a few enemies on that side too, of course… But the names don't mean anything to me. You're sure those are their real names?"

Flanagan shrugged. "Do we ever know?"

He started writing something down in his notebook. For several minutes there was silence in the room. Then Flanagan finished, and looked up at Mahood.

"There's only one more thing I have to ask you, Mr Mahood. Do you have a gun, for self-protection?"

Mahood hesitated a moment, then nodded.

"Can I see it?" asked the Guard.

Mahood got up and went to get the pistol from his bedroom. He returned and handed it to Constable Flanagan. The Guard took it and gave it a cursory inspection. "Mm," he said, "no sign that it's been fired recently. But I'll have to take it with me, I'm afraid, for forensics to look at… Again I have to point out, Mr Mahood, that you should have informed us that you were in possession of a gun. These things can't be treated lightly, you know…"

"I'm sorry, but I thought the fewer people who knew who I was the better…"

"It's actually illegal to hold a weapon without a licence… but, well, we won't talk about that now."

"So you're going to leave me without a gun?" said Mahood.

"It looks that way, doesn't it…? Why, were you intending to use it?"

Mahood felt his hackles rise again. "Quite possibly," he said, "especially since you say people are being shot at round here. I think I might have a right to protect myself."

"OK," Flanagan agreed, rising to his feet. "We'll get this back to you as soon as we can. But you'll have to make it legal. And if you feel you need something else in the meantime, you'll have to approach the proper authorities. If you call round at the police station in Donegal, they just might be able to help…"

He sounded very grudging. Clearly he didn't believe a word Mahood had said. But it didn't look as if he was going to take the matter any further, just at the moment. So Mahood nodded and said: "Thank you, I'd be grateful."

Flanagan was obviously reluctant to leave. His burly frame expanded as he took a deep breath.

"I have to say again, Mr Mahood, that it would have been better all round if you had contacted us in the first place about who you were. After all, these are not altogether settled times. And we're not so far from the North that we're immune from your troubles."

Mahood rose too. "No," he said, "I probably should have made contact. I'm sorry about that… But now you know."

Constable Flanagan gave him a last disdainful look, shook his hand briefly, and headed for the door.

As he opened it to let them out, Mahood asked: "What did Tony's mother, Kathleen, have to say about what happened on the mountain? I presume you questioned her too."

Constable Flanagan stopped on the doorstep and gave him a withering look.

"She said exactly the same as you," he said, with clear distaste. Then he turned and walked off down the track through the orchard.

Father Brian followed him quickly, without a word.

20

Tony Dougherty and a friend were shooting at each other from behind the gravestones.

Father Brian watched them as they ran from one Celtic cross to another. Tony's 'friend' was much younger than himself, maybe only six or seven. They were playing some game the young priest could not understand. They had stopped the shooting phase of their game and were now just clambering in and out of the headstones. It certainly didn't seem to be hide and seek, because neither of them was making any effort to hide. They were simply chasing each other round the stone memorials, occasionally laughing or shouting something inaudible.

Well bless them, he thought. It was good that someone was full of the joys of life.

His attention was drawn back to the matter in hand, saying farewell to the parishioners after the end of mass. He stood there shaking hands, exchanging greetings and comments on the weather, and in one case, with old Mrs Connelly, asking with as deep a concern as he could muster how she was getting on in the three weeks since her husband died.

When he had time to notice again, the two boys were still playing round on the far side of the graveyard.

Perhaps, thought Father Brian, Tony has heard about the chance of going to a new school, the special school in Sligo. That might explain why he was so full of beans. Yet he wondered if his mother had told him yet. In the last few days she had become very ambiguous about the whole thing. It was she, Kathleen, who had looked out the school, made inquiries about its reputation, about what the pupils did there, about how much it would cost, whether she could get some financial help, and so on. He had played only a peripheral role, supporting her application, recommending her as a worthy case, making a couple of phone calls to the directors.

Yet when the good news came through that her application had been successful, Kathleen suddenly seemed very lukewarm about the whole thing. She would miss her son, she had told him. Yes, Kathleen, I understand that, but it's for his own benefit. It'll do him a power of good.

But will they treat him decently? He's so difficult sometimes. They're bound to be irritated by his little ways. Would they, for example, allow him to go on copying out his characters…?

Don't worry, Kathleen, we'll keep the whole thing under review. He'll probably be right as rain. And if there is any problem, I'm sure they'll tell us. In the long run, he doesn't have to stay there. Only it's a tremendous opportunity. Not everyone can get into such a place…

As he shook another round of hands, he noticed her coming round the side of the chapel. She must have come out through the back of the church and along the side. A sudden, disappointing thought stood up in his mind. Was she trying to avoid him for some reason? He saw her glance over in his direction, then continue on her way, following Tony in among the gravestones, calling him.

Suddenly he felt a little deflated. He had to force himself to smile as the next batch of worshippers came out to take their leave of him. He found he was feeling more than a little upset. After all the support he had given her, after the time he had spent, almost alone among the villagers, counselling her over the problems with the two Tonys, senior and junior… was she now giving him the cold shoulder? He knew it was his priestly duty to look after his flock, in Christian love… and to seek no reward. She didn't have to be effusive about it, as so many people were with priests. But she could at least… well, just act in a friendly way. He might be a priest, but he was also a human being.

Kathleen had now reached Tony, coaxed him away from his young friend and led him to the churchyard gate. They disappeared through it without looking back towards the chapel.

His last parishioners had now departed, and Father Brian went back into the church to clear away before going for his lunch. As he took off his robes and put them carefully away in the vestry wardrobe, his mind remained with Tony. And with Kathleen. Another thought crossed his mind. Was she avoiding him, maybe, because she felt guilty about something?

Might it have something to do with the man Mahood?

He stopped for a moment, with his hand still on the handle of the wardrobe door. Then he shook himself. What suspicious thoughts are you allowing into your mind, Brian Dougan? Put an end to them now! You have absolutely no evidence of anything untoward in the relationship between Kathleen and Mahood. So why should you think it now? Was it because you were aware of people in the parish whispering about "the man in the house", and had assumed the gossip was linked with Kathleen? Come off it… Get down on your knees and ask for a clean heart!

Could it be, he wondered, resolving that he would indeed go and spend half an hour in prayer after his lunch, that such thoughts were linked with his jealousy of Mahood, over Tony?

He had become aware several weeks before, at the regatta, when he saw Mahood walking along the harbour mole side by side with Tony, that he was indeed jealous of the man. How long had he been in Killoole? A couple of months. And how long had he, Father Brian, tried to get on the same wavelength as Tony? The better part of a year. Yet he had never really succeeded in winning anything but a grudging acceptance of his friendship by the strange, introspective lad. While Mahood, well, he had seemed to strike it off with Tony straight away. And now it was known all round the village, that Kathleen Dougherty's lad had been 'taken in hand' by the new man, the gloomy, uncommunicative northerner from up at the big house.

Yes, Father Brian decided, he was suffering from a bout of childish jealousy, of a man who had beaten him to it in winning Tony's friendship! Well, there was only one thing to do with jealousy, and that was to throttle it at birth. Definitely a half hour of prayer after lunch, or maybe even an hour. And he shoved the wardrobe door firmly shut.

But he didn't leave the vestry. He stood there for some time, by the wardrobe, thinking. About Kathleen's strange behaviour, and her sudden coolness.

21

Later that day Father Brian was sitting in the confessional at one end of his church, still lost in thought.

He imagined he heard the side door of the chapel click shut, and waited for someone to enter the confessional. But nobody came. Ah well, perhaps it was just someone who'd come to pray in the sanctuary. Someone who knew the chapel was open at this time of day for confessions, but only wanted to pray alone. Sometimes that happened. Or sometimes they spent some time in prayer before approaching the confessional, by way of preparation. So he waited patiently, even though the time when he normally gave confession had already ended.

He often did a lot of thinking in the confession box, while he waited for people to come. And he settled back now and did so again. He had been thinking, before the interruption, about the funeral he had conducted the previous day. An elderly lady much loved in the community called Josephine Fox. She had appeared to be in good health, so her death came as a shock to most people. The day of the funeral had been grey and damp. And Father Brian had felt a huge burden of responsibility as he tried to find comforting words for the three daughters who had come with their spouses from Donegal and Sligo and Dublin. He hoped he had been able to be of some comfort, but he was very much aware that his words must have sounded conventional, rather stilted, a bit dry. Perhaps at least his sincerity had shown through...

He had lately been much preoccupied with death. It was not that it was something new for him. He had long been aware of the reality of death. Both his parents had died quite young, in their fifties. And professionally too he was not quite so innocent and unworldly as people in the village thought. His first posting after ordination had been in Belfast, to the Upper Falls in fact, as tough a parish as you could wish on anyone. And the older priests had not spared him. On the contrary, he soon realised that he was being sent on all the toughest assignments - mothers grieving for sons who had met a sudden and violent end; people who knew their brother or nephew or cousin was involved in the violence, but couldn't do anything about it; people who needed protection, and often demanded rather than requested that the church provide it - from the loyalists, from the security forces, from their own paramilitaries... and from all the brothers and nephews and cousins who were also part of it.

So he had been relieved, much relieved, when he was moved on after only eighteen months. Here it was much quieter, of course. But you also had more time to think, to ponder over it all, to reflect endlessly on all the harshness and pain. Yes, and also on the courage and kindness which came out in people, in the most unexpected circumstances. Like the fireman - Father Brian didn't know to this day if he'd been Catholic or Protestant - who went back into a burning house to save a child, only for the roof to collapse...

Here in Killoole people died relatively peaceful deaths, though that of course did little to diminish the suffering. If you died from a bullet, at least it was over and done with quickly. If you died from cancer in Donegal hospital it was slow and painful and long drawn out. For the grieving relatives there was not much consolation either way.

Yet that was his business - comforting those who faced death and those who were left behind after it. To bring to them a consciousness of God's love. He thought of all the people he had already tried to help as they faced the great divide leading to the unknown. He offered them words of hope and consolation, based on the teaching of the Church. But often he wondered what happened to those people. Where they really went. Was it credible that those personalities, so tied to their faces, their voices, their laughs and their little mannerisms, could live on without the bodies that gave their personality its form? Was it possible to believe that a person divorced from his or her body could be the same personality... could be a person at all?

Some people when they died were, sadly, only too forgettable. But others, from the very force of their personalities, would linger in your mind, your imagination, your memory for weeks, even for months. In some cases forever...

It was always the image of his mother that he clung on to. Her good-natured, gentle smile would stay in his mind until he died. But did that mean she had gone to a better place? Did it mean she was happily living in paradise, with all the other saints? He fervently hoped she was. He could not believe that a phenomenon so extraordinary as a person like her, an achievement of such complexity and wonder and goodness, so unique and irreplaceable... could simply disappear after the break-down of the body.

And yet, and yet... he found it difficult to imagine how, if the personality did live on, this could possibly be. Where did all those unique souls go? In what unimaginable domain, beyond place and time, did they dwell?

Often he fell asleep worrying about such things, pondering over them, and finding no answers...

His reflections were interrupted by another sound out in the sanctuary, by the sort of clunk a shoe makes against the wood of a pew. Father Brian looked at his watch. It was now a quarter past six. If there was someone still in the chapel it didn't look as if they were going to come anywhere near the confessional. So he stirred himself, said a brief prayer, and stepped out into the church.

It was growing dark outside, and the main doors were locked because of the weather. The small knave was lit by a single electric light above his head, near the confessional. Much of the sanctuary was in shadow. He peered towards the far end of the church, towards the side door which was left open exactly so that people could come and pray as they wished.

He saw no one, and turned towards the vestry.

Another muffled noise made him stop, and he turned again, just in time to see a figure slip from one of the darkened pews towards the side door. The nearby light made it difficult to see, but he thought he caught the dull gleam of a white shirt or blouse. Then the door opened and he saw the person silhouetted against the greyness of the ebbing day outside. Shortish hair. Couldn't make out the colour. Possibly sandy or blond. A man or a woman? He wasn't sure. From the quick movements Father Brian guessed it was a youngish person. But nobody he clearly recognised. And in a moment the door closed and the person was gone.

For a moment the priest thought of hurrying across the chapel in pursuit of the unknown worshipper. But he decided not to. It seemed undignified. And his main motive would have been curiosity, not any real desire to help.

He was intrigued nonetheless. If people came to his church they were usually not so secretive. Was it perhaps someone who wasn't used to coming into a church? Who hadn't been for a long time and felt awkward?

Someone, maybe, with something serious on their conscience, but who weren't at all sure they wanted to share it with a priest. Tormented by something they had done.

Or were about to do?

He heaved a sigh and decided to leave it. If the secret worshipper wanted to come back, no doubt they would do so in their own good time.

Nevertheless Father Brian went over to the window nearest the door and glanced out into the gathering gloom. The wet road leading down to the village was deserted.

Nothing except a few cars, and a dirty white van parked by the roadside.

22

The horizon that evening was a clear line between the rich red of the sky and the deep purple of the sea. An extraordinary sunset, Kathleen thought, as she stared out from the headland just above the village. The brooding mass of Slieve Trascart, to the right, looked down on a calm, almost mirror-like sea. A tiny tuft of mist clung to its summit, as if unwilling to part with the massive solidity of the mountain. The sky beyond was a complicated pattern of fishbone and furrows, lit from behind by the scarlet rays of an unseen sun.

For all the wonder and beauty of the scene, her mind was on other things. Tony had not come back for his tea. It was not the first time he'd stayed out this late. Several times before he'd gone off on some expedition with Shamie and Co., ending up in some deserted hut along the shore where they stayed for hours. Quite what they did there she could never fathom. But this time, for some reason, she felt more than her usual pangs of anxiety. This time, she sensed, it was much more serious. She was genuinely afraid for her son.

In the lane from her house to the main street she had met Dominic, the leader of the rival gang. A squat, graceless lump of a lad. She had asked him if by chance he knew if Shamie and his friends were out and about. He grunted something about not having seen them for days, and passed on. She had then done a tour of the harbour, but there was nobody there save a couple of youthful anglers, reluctant to admit that they would catch nothing that day. She had wandered to the eastern end of the village, past the intersection where the main street merged with the twisting lane coming down from the chapel. She'd even reached the lay-by where tourists liked to park their cars for the view over the village. But there was nobody about. Everyone was at home, or in the pub, or away in Castlecharles or Donegal.

Her anxiety grew. Small, disconnected shreds of the past, incidents from Tony's short life, kept flitting into her mind... She remembered the time when he was very young and she had taken him to the beach at Rossnowlagh, the long, broad beach where on a hot day there were hundreds of people. She had stopped to buy him an ice-cream at the single big hotel behind the beach. The woman serving had been slow, and when Kathleen turned away from the ice-cream stall there had been no sign of Tony. In panic she had run round the side of the building, shouting desperately. Everyone had turned to look at her. Then she had heard a thin wail and run round another corner. There was five-year old Tony, standing beside a perplexed woman with the same colour of dress as Kathleen. He was just standing there sobbing fitfully, his knees slightly bent, his eyes screwed up and his small fists beating the air helplessly. The sight had never left her.

...Now she was at the other end of the village, in the car park above the harbour, looking out along the westward shore towards the mountain. It was already too dark to hope to see much. But she scanned the dim outlines of the rocks and gullies anyway, in the vague hope of spotting something, a shadow perhaps, a movement which might give some clue to the whereabouts of her son.

Slowly her eyes turned up towards the gaunt silhouette of the old house on the Foreland.

She wondered. Tony and 'the man', as he had taken to calling him, had struck up a strange relationship. Could it be that he had somehow wandered up to the house and invited himself in? Yet Tony had been frightened of the house. Looking at the dark shapes of the house she suddenly felt a stab of fear. What if he was up there now...?

She began to walk quickly along the road round the inlet. Kathleen asked herself whether the fear she now felt had anything to do with the man, the unusual man who had come to live there. She now thought she knew all about him: who he was, what he was. She had a feeling that his presence in the village spelled danger. Since the day of the shooting on the mountain she had determined to have no more to do with him. Yet she felt sad at the thought. He had been correct, polite, had been kind to Tony. He had shown a lot more understanding of her son and his problems than most people in the village, the main exceptions being her neighbour Maureen and perhaps Father Brian. Something, she knew, must have brought this strange, sad man to their village. She wondered what it was.

Was she just being hopelessly romantic, but was there some hidden tragedy in the man's life?

She gave a little snort and told herself not to be so stupid. Then she looked up again at the old house. Something had caught her eye...

The red of the sunset had caught in some of its windows, giving it a strange, other-worldly look. For a fleeting moment she imagined she saw a face there, at one of the upper windows, turning its gaze mournfully down on her... It was only slowly, as she went on looking, that she realised that there was something not quite right about the house that evening. Normally she would have expected to see no more than a vague dark shape, a thicker blackness against an already darkening background. But the outline of the house was in a strange way silhouetted clearly against the darkness behind it. All the chimneys and gables were plainly visible against a ghostly red glow. A glow that had little to do with the sunset. Its source was somewhere behind the house.

She broke into a run, heading along the road towards Maeve's shop.

The big house was on fire!

The shop was closed, but when Kathleen hammered several times on the side door, Maeve appeared, bemused and frightened.

"Call the fire brigade, Maeve," she shouted. "The old house is on fire!"

And then she was off up the road towards the house itself.

As she drew nearer the flames became clearly visible, leaping up from the further side of the house. It must be a fierce fire, she thought, for the whole of the sky in that direction was now alight. She was struggling for breath, unused to running so far and so fast. She was at the iron gate, and on into the rutted drive that led up through the stunted orchard.

There were other people too. To her right she saw dark figures running in and out through the gnarled trunks of the fruit trees, coming from the houses further up the road. The house ahead of them now seemed to be burning fiercely, flames leaping high into the darkened sky around it. But Kathleen saw for the first time that it was only one side of the building which seemed to be on fire. The side away from the village.

The other side, looking down towards the village, the side with the main door, was untouched by the blaze.

As she ran up the last stretch through the apple trees she became conscious of a thick-set figure lumbering up the slope beside her. After a few moments she recognised who it was. Donal McManus, who lived up the lane on the other side of the road from here. He was stumbling along through the thick grass, wheezing from the unaccustomed effort. He was carrying a bucket in either hand.

"I've asked Maeve to ring the fire brigade, Donal."

He nodded. "It'll take them at least half an hour to get here from Rossinver," he muttered.

They turned round the side of the house and immediately winced at the heat of the blaze. Yet Kathleen felt a sudden wave of relief. She was not sure why. It was not the house itself that was on fire, but the wooden shed which lay on the far side of the sunken concrete yard. From the strange blue and yellow tints of the flames she guessed that the shed had stored something highly flammable, paint perhaps, or turpentine and methylated spirits. The blaze was fierce, frightening in its intensity. But so far it had not touched the big house itself.

Then she saw him, the house's owner, striding purposefully along the bank above the yard, talking to the line of people who had already gathered there, asking them to keep back, telling them there was nothing they could do. Then she heard his voice, assuring them in low, authoritative tones that the house was in no danger, that the hut was of no value and had only stored junk, that it was useless to try and put out the fire… Calm and confident, with none of the self-doubt and hesitation she had sensed on their previous meetings.

He stopped in front of her.

"Oh, hello. Thanks for coming, but I think everything will be OK. I don't think the house is in any danger."

He turned to the burly figure beside her.

"This is Donal," she said, "Donal MacManus."

"Yes," he said. "We met briefly, remember, at the regatta. Thanks for coming." And he held out his hand.

Donal took it, in silence. "You're not going to try to save the shed?" he asked in a gravelly voice.

Mahood shook his head. "It's not worth it. It's too far gone…"

But suddenly Donal was off, stumbling down the bank into the yard and headed for the tap which was plainly visible on the side of the house. Filling his buckets, he ran across the yard and began dousing down the already weakening flames. Soon he was joined by several others.

Kathleen suddenly remembered Tony.

"You haven't seen my son, have you?" she asked Mahood.

Again he shook his head. "I haven't seen him for days," he said, with a hint of regret. "Not since… we went to the mountain."

And he turned away to greet Father Brian, who was hurrying through the grass under the trees. The priest, however, ignored him and addressed himself to Donal, down in the yard.

"Do you think you should be doing that, Donal?" Father Brian called. "I mean, you might be spoiling evidence of how the fire started."

Donal ignored him, and went on throwing his buckets of water at the parts of the shed that were still burning.

The fire brigade came half an hour later, when there was nothing left to do. People were by now just standing round, staring at the glowing embers and charred upright poles which were all that was left of the shed.

"*You* haven't seen Tony this evening, have you, Father?" Kathleen asked the priest.

He looked at her curiously. "No, is he not at home?"

"He's been out all afternoon, and never came back for his tea… I wondered if you'd seen him with the other ones, Kieran and Shamie and those ones, up near the chapel. They sometimes hang out round there…"

"No… Well I did see Kieran… and Shelagh and Kevin were with him. But not Shamie, or your Tony… It's strange that he hasn't come home…"

She nodded glumly.

"I'll go and make enquiries," he said.

Flanagan the constable had arrived. He approached Mahood with a serious air.

"What was it that you stored in the shed?" he asked. "Everybody's saying it was quite a spectacular... conflagration."

Mahood smiled inwardly at the choice of words.

"To be honest, constable, I've hardly even been in the shed. Looked into it the first day I was here, just to see what was there, but I've never used it."

"And what was in there?"

"Oh, a lot of old junk. Old sofas and beds, and that sort of thing. And probably paint pots as well."

"So you haven't been doing any work in there? Say, with electrical equipment...?"

"No, no, nothing like that. As I say, I've never used the place..."

Mahood saw that people were drifting away, and realised this was an opportunity to meet some of them, and thank them.

"Would you all like to come into the kitchen?" he called. "The least I can do is offer you a cup of tea."

Donal, he saw, was making off slowly into the darkness with his two buckets. Mahood called after him.

"Would you not come in for a cup of tea?" he said. "Or something stronger, if you like?"

Donal stopped, and hesitated. Then he turned and came up to Mahood. The two were now alone, and evidently did not notice Kathleen, standing some distance away in the darkness.

"So are you going to come in then?" asked Mahood.

Donal shook his head. "No, I think it's best if I don't drink your whiskey, Mr Mahood," said Donal.

"You know, there's something very familiar about you, Mr... er McManus was it? Are you sure we haven't met? I mean, before the other day?"

Donal surveyed him coolly. "It's possible," he said slowly. "But in another life, another world... You understand?"

They looked at each other without speaking for a full minute. Then Mahood said:

"Yes, I understand."

"And there's something else you should understand," said Donal. "This fire was no accident."

Mahood's eyes narrowed.

"Do you know that? Or are you just guessing?"

Donal's face glowed red in the dying embers of the stricken hut.

"What exactly is it you're telling me, Mr McManus?" Mahood asked.

"It's a warning," said Donal, so faintly Kathleen hardly heard him.

"From you?" asked Mahood.

"No, not from me. But from someone else who knows you're here and knows who you are. And doesn't welcome you."

There was another pause. Then Donal said:

"You'd be foolish to ignore that warning, Mr Mahood." And he disappeared into the darkness.

23

The night before he left the house in Belfast where he had lived for twenty years, Mahood went into his daughter's bedroom and switched on the light.

Everything there was as it always had been, neat and tidy. Everything was in its place. The prim single bed with its light blue duvet. On the walls, highly coloured, sometimes lurid pictures of pop-stars whose names meant nothing to him. To one side the bookcase, with its colourful rows of videos and books, some of them just girly pulp, some of them more serious novels. And some of them books on foreign places... travel books, gazetteers, atlases. Those were her favourites. Also a few language books, though Deirdre had never progressed very far with the languages. Basically, Mahood reflected, she had been much too shy. Yet the languages, the peoples, the countries had fascinated her. She had wanted to travel, perhaps do something with her travels, maybe work for an aid agency...

There was a folder on the desk, neatly tied with a bright blue ribbon. Blue had always been Deirdre's favourite colour. Carefully, almost reverently, he untied it and looked down on the bits of paper inside.

There were some notebooks, including one plain school exercise book which had "My Diary" written on its cover. This was the first time he had realised she had tried to keep a diary... It seemed that it had lapsed after a couple of months, but had then restarted, not once, but three times. Two efforts when she was twelve, once at fifteen and then, very briefly, when she had been sixteen.

Much of it was predictable. School gossip. Cinema trips with friends. Malicious comments about girl friends, and a few boys... And then, just a few times, an attempt to analyse her own thoughts and motivations...

"Do I really want to work if I go travelling? Often I think I would much rather just wander with friends in the cities with their temples, the mountains and forests with their baboons and tigers, or laze on a beach under the palm trees. But I suppose

you can't just travel if you don't earn money. Also, I suppose there would be plenty of dangers there too. People just waiting to cheat or rob (or, shock, horror... murder?) young idiots like myself..."

At the end of one of the notebooks he came across a detailed description of a country he had never heard of. There were statistics: area, population, capital city, languages spoken... And a very carefully drawn, extremely detailed map. Yet he didn't recognise it as any country he had ever heard of.

Its name was Borovsaat, and a note underneath this word informed him that the name meant (in the Borovian language) "The Country behind the Mountain"...

The next few pages were devoted to the history of Borovsaat, and its age-long enmity with the island kingdom of Rovonia, an archipelago off the coast of Borovsaat largely covered in forests, many of them apple groves...

He closed the notebook quickly and was about to close the folder too. But then he saw the letter, the letter from Scotland.

He remembered receiving it. Deirdre had longed to travel far and wide. But Scotland was as far as she had ever gone. With a school trip to the Highlands. For a week.

She had written to him from there. At least, she had written to both her parents, but some of the references in the letter were intimately related to things that only she and he had talked about. Deirdre had not been consciously excluding her mother, but he wondered if Catriona had had any clue what her daughter was talking about sometimes. He decided that his wife could not have read the letter properly, since she had not asked for any explanation of things she could not possibly have understood.

"Monday 17th August. Craiglochie... Dear Old Things," Deirdre had written. This was her idea of being irreverent and yet affectionate. *"Guess what! It rains in Scotland as well! And they have mountains... at least I'm told they have. We haven't seen them yet, because of the cloud. We're taking bets. How many days will it be before we see the top of Sgur Mor, which is the big mountain you're supposed to see from the hostel. The favourite, by a long way, is 'Not before we leave'!*

I've been a bit more optimistic, though. I put my bet, at 20/1, on 'The day before we leave, in hot sunshine!' I can just imagine it. At the head of the valley, where there's nothing at the moment but thick fog and heavy rain, the clouds will miraculously open and there it will be! A high, conical peak with craggy bits on the top, bathed in glorious sunshine, covered with purple heather and with wild mountain torrents streaming down its side: Sgur Mor!...

Thursday 20th.

Well, we've finally seen it. Sgur Mor, that is. Up until then I had the impression that behind the mountain there could only be some great boiling pit, full of a grim, grey fuming broth - because what else could explain why the clouds come continually pouring over it, grey and cold and full of rain. Then finally, last night, when we got back from our hopelessly wet and boggy hike, it was there! I got up to our room in the hostel and it was... well, almost as I had imagined it. A bit less craggy, but with enough jagged bits to make it look quite exciting...

And there was this strange glow from behind it, a sort of mixture of rose and peach. And it made me revise my ideas about what must be behind the mountain. I decided the great grim pot of boiling cloud was just a myth, a bad dream. Behind the mountain, I decided, there's another wide valley, like the one we're in. Only this one is, if anything, more beautiful. There are forests leading down to a ragged, rocky coastline round a long inlet of the sea. And small villages of white cottages. And the sun always seems to be rising there, over the low, lumpy mountains on the far side of the valley. And as it warms the waters of the inlet a mist rises and forms the clouds that float over into our valley, here on the nearside of the mountain. That's why there's always rain here, but there... on the other side... nothing but sunshine and warmth and a feeling of belonging..."

Frankie had been on the phone again.

"MacManus, I've found out who your guy Mahood is."

"Oh yeah..."

"He was in the CID..."

"I sort of reckoned that."

"Supposedly retired three or four months ago, not long after an incident just off the M1. You must have heard of it... Some of the 'comrades' tried to grab Baird, you know, the spokesman for Security, and it went badly wrong. Aye, that one... Three of our lads, you may remember, got it in the neck... Now Mahood was involved in that. And the boys, to put it mildly, are a bit pissed off about the whole thing, what with our lads getting done and all... So this Mahood is not a very popular guy around these parts, if you take my meaning..."

"What, did Mahood shoot all three himself or something?"

"No, no, maybe one of them. But he was on the scene. Very much involved. Senior man on the spot, so to speak. And then he suddenly retires. Funny, isn't it?"

"So why did he retire?"

"Well the question is: did he? Some think he got sacked because it was such a balls-up, from their point of view as well as ours. Couple of civilians got shot up in the crossfire... And there are those that think Mahood's not retired really at all, that it's all just a smokescreen, to get him out of the way for a while, until the heat over this thing cools off. Either that or they might be preparing him for something special. You know, something undercover or the likes. What better place to hide him than to send him down to some remote place... like a village in Donegal to study the wildlife and maybe pick up a few tips about 'fraternising with the enemy'? So... if you're sure that your guy down in... what's the place called where you are?..."

"Killoole."

"If your guy down in Killoole really is Mahood, then some people round here might just be a little bit interested."

"Ehe... Look, Frankie, I hope you don't mind my asking this, but..."

"No, Donal, don't even think about it. Don't dare to set foot back in Belfast for twenty years at least!"

"No, I wasn't going to say that. What I was going to ask is that you don't say too much about this to your... contacts, you know. I mean, I don't buy all this bullshit about 'undercover work' and all that. What if the guy really has just retired and wants to get away from it all...?"

There was a low chuckle from Frankie's end of the line. "What's happening, Donal? You going soft? Get away from it all, indeed... Maybe you really did let that little f***** Micky Walsh get out the back door!"

"No, Frankie, for f***** sake don't talk like that! It's just... well, I don't want those guys coming over to this part of the world. I just phoned to ask about Mahood, not to inform on him or anything..."

"It's a bit late now, Donal. The informing's been done, if you see what I mean. But don't worry about it! Look, if this guy really is involved in something 'hush-hush', if you know what I mean, won't the boys at the top be grateful to you? They won't want to take it out on you, will they?"

Donal said nothing. He was already regretting having phoned Frankie in the first place.

24

Kathleen took another sniff at the shirt. Yes, definitely a hint of something chemical. Turpentine maybe. Her blood ran cold. What had Tony been doing with turpentine?

He was busy copying his signs. Or rather studying them. He had taken of late to writing individual characters and then looking for them in the little plastic-backed book that Mr Mahood had brought back from Dublin or Belfast or somewhere. *"A Chinese-English Pocket Dictionary"* it said on the cover. The book had baffled Tony at first. He didn't seem to associate it with the characters which he copied out so painstakingly, and after a day or two he had abandoned it, leaving it unopened on the sitting room dresser. But just in the last week, she noticed, he had taken it up again, and had even copied out some of the characters in it, though he said they were not written in quite the same way as the ones in the newspaper. Nevertheless, he now seemed to have established that there was a connection between the book and the newspaper, though sometimes it seemed to take him literally hours to find characters which corresponded between them.

"Tony, what have you got on your shirt sleeve? Here, this bit that smells… What is it?"

Tony turned away, concentrating even more on the character he was examining. His mother looked down at him, with an expression of worry and fear.

"You still haven't told me where you were the other night. The night there was the fire…"

He still didn't look at her.

"I didn't see no fire," he said plaintively. He had never been a good liar.

Kathleen put the shirt in a plastic bag and left Tony to his devices. She put on her coat and went out the back door, locking it carefully behind her. Tony would be all right. He knew not to answer the door if anyone came.

She had decided to go to the only person she thought might be able to help her.

It was late, and Father Brian was just saying good bye to the ladies taking part in the bingo session in the parochial hall. But he was friendly, and clearly glad to see her. He shut up the hall, chatting away cheerfully about nothing in particular, and led her back to the presbytery.

His demeanour changed when she showed him the shirt. He sat down heavily in an armchair by the fireplace. After a few moments he began to speak. His voice was tired and disappointed.

"I cross-questioned most of the others. Shamie and Dominic and all the older ones. They all seem to have an alibi... So I've been going round saying it must have been someone from outside the village. Possibly something to do with Mahood's criminal connections in the North..."

She was a little shocked at the hostility towards Mahood that she sensed in the priest's voice. She had thought Father Brian felt some sympathy towards him. She had even heard some gossip about the two drinking together. 'Is it right to be drinking with a stranger?' she had heard Maeve Meahan ask a customer. 'And we don't even know who the man is...'

"What do you think it is on the shirt?" Kathleen asked timidly.

Father Brian shook his head. "Turps, no doubt about it."

He paused.

"What is it?" she asked, alarm in her voice.

"Well I... I have to tell you this, Kathleen. I heard Mahood telling Constable Flanagan that there was paint and turpentine in the shed..."

A clock began to chime in the hall outside. Ten o'clock.

"What should we do?" she asked quietly.

Father Brian shook his head a second time, but said nothing.

At that moment there was a knock on the door and the housekeeper appeared. "I have someone to see you, Father," she said.

"Not now, Mrs O'Donnell, can't you see we're in the middle of something?"

"But I think it's to do with that," said Mrs O'Donnell grimly. She opened the door wider, and Tony advanced nervously into the room.

"Tony!" exclaimed Kathleen. "How did you get out of the house?"

He looked at her reproachfully.

"I know where the key is. The one you hide on the kitchen dresser. Behind the egg cups."

Her mouth fell open, but she said nothing.

"And why have you come, Tony?" asked the priest. "Why have you come without your mother's permission?"

"I wanted to tell you something," he mumbled.

Father Brian looked at him sternly but gently.

"You can speak in front of your mother, Tony," he said.

"No, I only want to tell it to you," Tony answered.

Kathleen was angry now.

"Tony, there's no way I'm going to..."

But she caught the young priest's eye. He smiled at her apologetically.

"Perhaps it's best if Tony and I just have a moment together, Kathleen," he said. "I'll call you in again in a minute or two."

She wanted to rebel, to say no. But then she thought better of it and rose to go. As she passed Tony she ruffled his hair, then hurried out.

"What is it you wanted to tell me, Tony?" asked Father Brian when she had gone. Tony had sat himself down without an invitation on the large sofa.

Tony did not answer immediately. He seemed to be thinking deeply.

"Did you want to tell me something about the fire?"

Tony screwed up his face, as if concentrating hard. Then he asked:

"The house wasn't burned down, was it?"

The priest shook his head.

"And can they put you in prison for burning down just a shed?"

Father Brian gave the boy a severe look.

"If someone did it deliberately… and they were old enough, yes, they might put him in prison. Or fine him a lot of money."

"But Mr Mahood never used that shed. I know, he told me so."

"But Tony… that doesn't excuse someone burning it down."

Tony thought again.

"Priests aren't supposed to tell the police things, are they?"

Father Brian winced. "Well, that only applies to things they hear in the confessional, Tony…"

"I only did it to scare him away!"

Father Brian stood up slowly and went to the door. He opened it slowly, but there was no one outside. He heard voices from the kitchen. Kathleen Dougherty had evidently gone to talk to Mrs O'Donnell. He closed the door and came back to his armchair.

"Why did you want to scare him away, Tony? I thought he had been kind to you… Did he not buy you a little book recently, as I was hearing?"

Tony nodded.

"And you liked the book, your mother says…"

Tony said nothing.

"And at one stage, I know, you liked Mr Mahood too."

Tony looked up.

"Do you like Mr Mahood, Father?"

The priest looked out the window, at the gathering dusk.

"Yes, I think I do, Tony. He's not a bad man at all…"

"But Shamie and Kieran say the Protestants should go. They should all leave Ireland."

Father Brian shook his head. "No, no, no, Tony. That's all nonsense. There's room here for everyone, and we should try to live in peace with our Protestant neighbours…"

"But I don't want him marrying my Mam," said Tony vehemently.

Father Brian's eyes opened wide, and then he gave a little laugh. "I don't think, Tony," he said quietly, "I don't think there's any chance of that. Really. Has your Mam ever...? Has she ever even gone out with him?"

Tony shook his head.

"I didn't think so," said the priest.

"But they like each other," said Tony, "and Mammy is so lonely. I just don't want it to happen. All the others would laugh at me!"

Father Brian looked hard at Tony and saw all the emotion that was welling up inside the boy. He was totally lost for words.

"The man has made the village unhappy," said Tony. "He's made my Mam unhappy."

Father Brian began to nod his head up and down, very slowly.

"Yes, Tony," he said simply. "I know what you mean."

"Will you tell anyone I did it," asked Tony after a pause.

"No, Tony. You can be sure I won't."

25

Mahood gave up waiting after an hour and a half. Angrily, he slipped the car into gear and prepared to turn out of the rough parking space. It was the same place he had used for his first rendezvous with McFaul. It was a better evening than that first time. No rain or mist, and there were even some clear patches of blue sky over to the west. And yet the clouds overhead, in marked contrast, were heavy and threatening.

McFaul must have been held back by some urgent case. Mahood wasn't surprised. It wasn't easy for policemen to get away, especially when they were under investigation for involvement in not just one, but two separate shootings.

A pity. He had really wanted to discuss the situation with McFaul. And he could have done with the company. He had been tempted to arrange the rendezvous in one of the pubs they had used before, a suitable distance from Killoole. But after the shooting on the mountain he knew that it wasn't just paramilitaries he had to elude. The Gardai were keeping an eye on him too. So he had chosen the same remote spot in the middle of a mountain bog to make it easier for both of them to detect pursuit.

But this time the wait had made him even more nervous. Mahood kept looking down at where his right hand rested lightly on the steering wheel. It had hardly stopped its nervous tapping since he got there. And when it stopped tapping, it went on moving. It fidgeted, it shook, it made vague, jerky movements in the air. He just couldn't keep it still.

Mahood had known sadness before, and plenty of grief. But he had never experienced anything like what he was going through now. It was as if he had been making his way across an open field, with no obstruction greater than a thistle or two, and had walked slap bang into an invisible wall. He had thought things were beginning to get easier in the village. A few people now greeted him. There seemed to be a grudging acceptance from the others. But then came the incident on the mountain, followed by the fire. Neither incident had shaken him at the time. The old adrenalin, no doubt, had kept him calm and businesslike. He had kept his cool when

Constable Flanagan and the priest had questioned him. He had kept his cool during the fire, unlike some of the villagers. He had even slept well for two nights afterwards, something that hadn't happened for months.

But after a few days things began to change. The two incidents, in quick succession, had obviously set off some malign mechanism within him which he didn't understand and couldn't control. Suddenly when he tried to make a cup of coffee his hands were shaking. When he wanted to go down to the village his knees would go weak. When he woke up in the morning he would have a splitting headache. He would be sitting at the kitchen table reading a football report in the paper, and find he'd been sitting there for twenty minutes and hadn't taken in a thing.

And his thought processes were now totally out of control. It was the memories that were the worst. There was no way of keeping them at bay. They just kept flashing up in his mind without warning. Totally unexpected memories, of things he thought he'd completely forgotten. Memories not just of his daughter. Some were of his own childhood. Of the death of a particularly beloved aunt, also sudden and unexpected. Funnily enough, Sally had been the aunt who never gave him and his sisters any sweets or sticky buns. But they had loved her anyway, for her dry sense of humour and sarcastic smile... There were memories of his own happy hours as a child on a beach, at Bangor or Portrush. Of visits to an uncle's farm. Of singing in an unknown church, perhaps at Sally's funeral, and the patterns formed on the white walls as bright sunlight played through the stained glass.

But the memories of Deirdre were the worst. Sudden, painful, relentless...

Mahood took one last look along the road to the east, then swung the car in the opposite direction and headed for home. All the way across the bog, along the twisting valley road, down into the village, he fought against his new demons, the laughing, mocking demons which took the form of happy faces and places from his past life. If he gave in to them, he knew, he might lose control of himself altogether. Indeed, at one point he was so overcome by emotion that he started to look for some stopping place on the narrow road, a gateway or a farm entrance, where he could sit and recover.

But there was none, so he was forced to drive on. He plunged into the deep wooded glen on the last stretch before the village. Mahood knew he was driving erratically. At the last sharp bend round a buttress of rock he misjudged his speed and swung out too far. The heavy lorry labouring up the hill stopped in its tracks, too cumbersome to take evasive action. Mahood swerved at the last moment and must have missed the massive metal fender by inches. He slid on down the road, trying not to hear the angry blare of the lorry's horn.

At last he reached the crossroads above the village and continued down the winding road towards the Foreland. Almost home! he thought with a wry smile on his face. What a home!

As he turned off the road he found to his astonishment that the iron gate was wide open. He was sure he had closed it when he left. And as he drove on up the track to the house he turned one of the corners and nearly ran down a tall figure climbing laboriously up the slope. He stopped and opened the car window. It was Father Brian.

"Get in," he said. "I'll take you up... I presume you were looking for me?"

The priest nodded, and got in.

When they reached the bleak hallway, with its high ceiling and steep staircase, Mahood noticed the priest was carrying a bottle of whiskey.

"A peace offering," said Father Brian, holding it out to him.

Mahood raised his eyebrows. "Were we ever at war?" he asked.

He led the way into the sitting room and turned on the lamp beside the fireplace. The embers of last night's turf fire lay cold and dusty in the grate. Mahood threw several logs on to the ashes, hoping it would retake. Until it did, he thought, the whiskey would have to provide them with some inner warmth.

"Where have you been?" asked the priest.

Mahood didn't reply for a while. Finally he said:

"I was looking for someone."

Father Brian didn't seem to find anything strange about this reply. He thought a moment and then said:

"You're sure you weren't trying to avoid someone who was looking for you?"

Despite himself Mahood smiled. He poured out two glasses of whiskey.

"Maybe that as well," he said, handing one glass to the priest. "I've been doing that for as long as I can remember… I'm tired of doing that."

They sat down in front of the fire. Mahood noted with satisfaction that a small flame had begun licking one of the logs.

"Is that one of the reasons you came here?" asked the priest quietly.

Mahood took a sip of his whiskey and nodded slowly. "I suppose so. Yes, it was one of the reasons."

"And who is it who's been looking for you? Republicans? The IRA? I would have thought that if you're trying to get away from them, you may have come to the wrong place."

Mahood pondered for a few moments. Then he answered.

"It's not just the Republicans I've been trying to get away from."

Father Brian raised his eyebrows.

"There were people on the other side who had it in for me too. A question of the loyalists seeing me as a traitor to their cause. Some of the loyalists, you know, hate us as much as the republicans do. Maybe more so. The republicans were brought up hating us, so they've sort of got used to it. To them we're just something that stands in their way, something to be got rid of. And in their cocky way they're so confident they'll succeed that they sometimes laugh at us more than they hate us. The loyalists, on the other hand, are furious that we don't let them just have a go at the republicans… And there was one group of loyalists that I and a friend pissed off in particular. It was probably them who had a go at me on Slieve Trascart… as you've probably guessed."

The priest stared at his whiskey for a while.

"It still seems a strange thing to do, to come to west Donegal to 'get away' from the violence. Are you sure there weren't other reasons for coming here? Could it be that you weren't so much 'getting away from it' as looking for someone in particular… someone from your past?"

Mahood, slouched low in his chair, raised his eyes and gave the priest a curious look. Father Brian thought he caught a glimpse of irritation, but then saw it change quickly into something else. There was a hint of mild amusement. But behind it a deeper sadness.

"Maybe you're right," Mahood murmured, turning his eyes towards the brightening glow of the rekindled fire. "Maybe I was looking for someone…"

Father Brian waited for him to go on, but Mahood volunteered no more. So finally the priest plucked up courage and asked the question.

"So who is it that you're looking for?"

Mahood pulled a face and took a mouthful of whiskey. "I think, Father Brian, you're too used to people revealing all in the confessional. You forget that I'm not one of your tribe. My secrets are my own, between me and my maker…"

It was Father Brian's turn to feel irritation. There was a hint of mockery in the man's words. And more than a hint of rejection of his peace feelers. For a moment he regretted coming here with his "offering." But the moment passed, and he said gently:

"I think sometimes people have secrets that they have to share with others, as well as the Almighty. It's come to my ears, and not, I may add, at the confessional, that you go off at strange hours of day and night. Are you looking for something? Are you meeting someone?"

Father Brian had meant to provoke Mahood, challenge him, force him to reveal just a little more about himself. He was surprised by the effect his words had. There was not the angry rebuttal he had expected. Mahood's features became troubled, distant, concerned. And finally they twisted into a rather forced and unnatural smile. He leaned forward in his armchair.

"Yes, perhaps I am looking for someone, as I said. Perhaps I am meeting someone… But not in the sense I think you mean. Could I ask you a favour? Could we drop this subject? I don't want to find myself telling you untruths just to cover up things I can't even begin to describe to you. You… deserve better than that."

Then he leaned back and swallowed the remnants of the whiskey in his glass.

"Have another?" he asked Father Brian, indicating the glass. He seemed to have forgotten the whiskey belonged to the priest.

"No thanks," replied the priest, perplexed by what Mahood had just said. Then, after a moment, he spoke again.

"I apologise," he said, "for appearing to pry. I know it's not my business… I suppose I thought I might be able to offer advice. But could I ask you just one more thing, and ask for an honest reply? Do you know, or have you ever heard of, a man called Donal McManus?"

Mahood's eyes narrowed. He thought for a while, and then he said: "Yes, I've met him a couple of times. Heavy fellow. Probably drinks too much."

"Did you know he was once a key man in a paramilitary group, in one of the Belfast brigades?"

Mahood had been pouring himself another drink, but stopped.

"So that's why he seemed a bit familiar… Never met him before, but I may have seen a mug shot somewhere."

The priest didn't respond to this, but asked another question.

"Is he the person you came here to look for?"

Mahood looked at him as if he hadn't understood the question. Then a slow smile crossed his face.

"No," he said, "no no, it was someone totally different I came to find."

"Someone local? From the community here?"

Mahood shook his head.

"Someone from the North, like yourself, who's settled here?"

The retired policeman thought for a moment, and smiled, a curious, gentle smile. "Yes, I think maybe they have. Somewhere near here."

26

Yes, thought Mahood to himself after the priest had gone, I did have a rendezvous with someone here. But there was no way I could have explained it to this young man, shepherd of souls as he may be. A pity. He meant well and he deserved a fuller answer.

So my meetings with McFaul have been observed, he thought. Or at least the fact that I have been meeting somebody. Better be a bit more careful. Don't want to involve McFaul any more than can be helped.

But what *had* happened to McFaul that evening? Why had he not turned up at the meeting place? Why had he not phoned? The arrangement had been clear enough. Same place as the first meeting. Five o'clock. But McFaul hadn't come. Was McFaul himself in some trouble - this unlikely ally who was about the only person he could rely on?

The man who had been at his side on that fateful night five months before...

Mahood had known McFaul for years. But it was quite by chance that their paths had crossed on that particular night, a night which was to bind them in a grim brotherhood for what was left of their lives.

They had known each other for years, but were hardly friends. McFaul was known in the station as a member of one of the smaller and stricter denominations, a Baptist or Plymouth Brethren. That made Mahood keep his distance. Not that McFaul was unpleasant or unfriendly. He was amicable enough, in a subdued sort of way. But the fact that he was some sort of bible pusher, that's what had made Mahood wary. Religion was all very well, but you didn't want it pushed down your throat every day of the week.

They rarely worked together on cases. But back at the station, after a stressful day, McFaul was often the one who had the time and patience to listen for five minutes as Mahood blew off a head of steam over some unpleasant incident on the street. And when they left the station for home each evening - in a carefully orchestrated operation involving the watch-tower and the man on the gates - Mahood and McFaul would often leave together. McFaul lived in the same general direction as Mahood, only a few miles further from the city centre. And more and more in recent years Mahood had tended to invite him for a quick drink and chat at the Castlehill Arms, a small and safe hostelry off the Lisburn Road, before they finally made their way home.

It was a surprise for Mahood when McFaul first accepted. He didn't think that Plymouth Brethren, if that was what he was, were allowed to visit pubs. Evidently he was wrong, though McFaul did tend to go for something light, a shandy or light ale, rather than the whiskey that Mahood preferred. McFaul was clearly not quite as strict in his views as the station generally believed. And when he thought about it, Mahood realised he had never heard McFaul express any particularly strong views on religion. His political comments, what's more, were limited to a few mildly ironic asides aimed at politicians from both sides of the great divide. Certainly nothing strong enough to provoke an angry response from his companions - particularly not from Mahood, who had long since given up expressing any political or religious views.

And then McFaul had been taken off to do some specially 'hush-hush' work, or that was what the buzz was. One colleague said they thought it had something to do with ferrying VIPs around the province, a special 'bodyguard patrol' as he put it.

And after McFaul had gone, Mahood found he missed the man's company. Though they had never exactly been friends, Mahood had grown used to the man's steadiness, the unflappability of his manner, his ability to remain calm when everyone else in the station was going mildly berserk.

So they had not seen each other for seven or eight months before the night in question...

The evening had begun for Mahood with an argument, an argument at home. When Mahood looked back on it, the worst thing was that it had been his fault. Or at least, he could easily have prevented the argument from happening.

It was one of those comparatively rare evenings when Mahood was able to share a meal with his wife and daughter. And though none of them was very talkative at the table, the time had passed pleasantly enough. That is, until the subject of the ear-rings came up. Deirdre's new boyfriend wore ear-rings.

When Mahood first saw them he was sorely tempted to say something sarcastic. But he made a huge effort, bit his lip and said nothing. In recent years that had become his way of dealing with things. Just ignore them and wait for them to go away. For several weeks he had kept his peace. He had even, in a way, come to accept the situation. But that particular evening Deirdre began to recount how the office manager at the insurance company where she and Vernon worked had actually ordered... yes, ordered Vernon to take off his ear-rings. It was against company policy, he told him.

"Vernon just said: 'I can't'," said Deirdre, spluttering with laughter. "Just like that. 'I can't because they're stuck in!' You should have seen the man's face, he said..."

And she and her mother had dissolved in helpless laughter.

Again Mahood bit his lip. This time quite literally.

But finally he said: "And you don't feel any sympathy for the manager?"

He said it in as mild a way as he could. But the laughter stopped abruptly. They both looked at him.

"Sympathy with what?" asked Deirdre coolly.

"Well most work places have a dress code."

They were looking at him as if he were from another planet.

"Yes?" Deirdre challenged him.

Then Catriona said: "Is there really anything so extraordinary about a young man wearing ear-rings? In this day and age?"

It was her tone that annoyed him. That and the fact she was siding with their daughter. Yes, he was actually jealous of that. That had always been his prerogative. He and Deirdre had always been the pals when she was little. But no longer.

He also knew he couldn't rationalise his feelings.

"Yes," he said quietly. "Men with ear-rings are trying to make a statement... And a provocative statement."

That was how the row began. It was short and violent and uncompromising. And he was in the minority. Catriona was worse than Deirdre, firing at him any low-level shots she thought would hurt him.

"I thought you would have approved of him," she chided. "After all, he's a Protestant, isn't he? Son of a minister too."

She always treated him, in her oh so righteous Scottish way, as if he were the world's worst religious bigot. Which was very unfair, and she knew it. But she taunted him anyway, just to anger him.

"I don't care what he is," he fired back. "I'd prefer a decent Catholic to a guy with ear-rings... He probably has rings on other parts of his body too!"

At this point Deirdre rose from the table, her face a burning red. A moment later the front door slammed behind her.

He felt immediately that he wanted to apologise. For some reason, that particular night, he didn't want her to be angry with him. He cursed himself and the malign gift of sarcasm which had marked him all his life.

And was to leave an indelible scar on his soul forever after.

27

Mahood was still seething with anger and remorse when the phone went. It was barely half an hour since Deirdre had walked out, and Catriona was playing super-loud music in the kitchen. Some smooth orchestral music, but played at such a level as to be doubly irritating. All the while Mahood's heart had been pumping so heavily that he'd been unable to settle down. He had been on the point of grabbing his coat and going out to look for Deirdre, when the phone, half hidden under the line of coats by the door, shuddered and burst into a shrill cry.

"Yes," he muttered angrily into it.

"Mahood?"

"Yes."

"Get your coat on man. We have an emergency."

"What's happened?"

"Get down to the motorway, to the intersection near you! Someone's tried to ambush Baird…"

"Baird, the spokesman on security?"

"The very one…"

"So who's…?"

"Look, we haven't time for questions. Just get down there! But be careful. There's been shooting and at least one of our men is down. But they have the guys cornered, just by the underpass. They think. But Mahood…"

"Yes…"

"There's a complication. A couple of civilians have got involved. Their car was hit by the terrorists as they were trying to escape with Baird…"

"They've got Baird!"

"Yes, but they haven't got away. Our guys say the bad guys' car is a write-off…"

Mahood slammed down the phone. Catriona, his wife, appeared on the stairs.

"Is it about... Deirdre?" she asked anxiously.

He shook his head as he struggled into his coat. "No, there's been an attack on a Unionist politician. Just down the road..."

"Be careful," she called nervously as he went out the door.

Mahood knew it was time to stop when he came to a haphazard clutch of cars parked pell-mell across the road. The suburban residences came to an end here, and the road curled round a shoulder of parkland topped by a copse of pine trees. Round that corner, he knew, the road descended to the roundabout which led on to the motorway.

"There's been a shooting!" one of the cars' drivers called to him as he stopped his car and got out on to the pavement. There was a group of them, gathered in a little knot by the roadside.

"It's still going on," another one said. "I wouldn't go any closer if I were you."

Mahood took out his police badge and flashed it at them. Beyond the huddle of cars he spied a constable in uniform.

"What's the situation?" he asked, recognising the man as Hutchison, from the neighbouring station.

"It's a bit confused, sir... Bryson, from special branch, is up there at the trees above the corner. He'll be able to brief you better."

Mahood made his way up the slope to the clump of trees looking down on the intersection. There were two armed policemen among the pines along with Bryson. Mahood gave him a quick handshake. Bryson spoke in a tense whisper.

"One of the terrorists' cars cut out across Mr Baird's vehicle, and then the other tried to block it from behind. But Baird's chauffeur rammed the first one and must have injured the driver... Anyway, they tried to take Mr Baird off in the second one, but just at that moment this other car, couple of civilians came racing down the hill here and collided with the terrorists' second car. That's when one of our patrol cars arrived - Baird's driver must have called for help - and the shooting started. Some of the attackers were badly injured, but at least one of them has made off into the undergrowth. He took at least two people with him. One we think is Baird, and the other is someone from the unknown car..."

For the first time an alarm bell began to ring in Mahood's mind.

"Who were the civilians?"

"I don't know for certain, but the driver's still stuck in the car. Must be badly injured... It was the passenger that the gunman took with him."

Mahood was staring down the hill. Cars were still whizzing past on the motorway overpass beyond the intersection, speeding off out of the city. But he saw that two police cars had already sealed off the access and exit roads leading down to the roundabout beneath. On that roundabout, in the shadow of the overpass, four cars were locked in a deadly embrace. One was a sleek black limousine, two others were medium-range saloons. And one was a small Fiat, pale green in colour.

That was the one that caught his eye first.

Mahood was suddenly running down the grassy bank, past the neatly tended flower beds. He heard Bryson shout to him:

"What are you doing, Mahood? They have guns, they're still out there..."

Mahood wasn't listening. He was heading straight across the carefully mown grass, on to the tarmac of the road, heading for the small green Fiat. He reached the first pair of enmeshed cars and almost stumbled on a figure bent double, leaning over something prostrate on the ground. He heard almost simultaneously a moan and an oath.

"It's OK," he said quickly. "I've come to help..."

"Mahood!" came a low reply. "What the f*** are you doing? I could have shot you..."

"OK, Thompson, don't get in a lather... Are you OK?"

"It's just a nick on the arm, but it's bloody painful," said Thompson.

"Who have you got here?" asked Mahood tensely, nodding to the prone figure on the ground.

"Baird," said Thompson grimly.

"He going to be OK?"

"Dunno… He's got a bullet in his shoulder and he's in pain. Passed out a moment ago. Says at least one of them got away. And he took Baird's bodyguard, the chauffeur, at gunpoint. You know him, the bodyguard. It's McFaul, who used to be at your station…"

Mahood nodded grimly. There was a body spread-eagled by the car next to the limousine, and at least two dark shapes slumped near the one by the Fiat. That meant, he reckoned, there was probably only one of the abductors still at large.

"Bryson said they took someone else too."

"Yes. Someone from that little green car."

"Male or female?"

Thompson looked at him curiously. "I've no idea," he said. "But he took them into the allotments over there…"

He nodded towards the dark space on the other side of the roundabout.

"He took just one person apart from the bodyguard? Just one?"

"How many times do I…?" Thompson began irritably. "Yes, I *think* so. That's what Baird said."

Mahood bent down and ran across to the second pair of cars. The small green Fiat had rammed the raiders' car right in the middle of one side, and turned it half over.

Mahood reached the Fiat's door and, taking a deep breath, glanced inside.

There, sprawled over the wheel with his face turned in Mahood's direction, was Vernon, Deirdre's boyfriend. For some reason the first thing Mahood saw was the ear-ring glinting in the semi-darkness. He also saw that he wouldn't have to disapprove of poor Vernon any longer. His nose had been crushed by the impact and his mouth was still dripping blood. Vernon's eyes were wide open, but Mahood saw at once that he was dead.

The passenger seat beside him was empty.

Mahood crouched behind the damaged frame of his daughter's car. Then he leant against its side and shuddered. No, this couldn't be happening. He had witnessed many nightmares in his twenty odd years in the service. But they had been other people's nightmares. Not his own.

Bryson arrived at his side a moment later. "Have you gone mad?" he demanded, pulling Mahood down behind the shelter of the vehicle. "If the hijackers weren't going to shoot you, then our guys might well have done it for them! There's an alert still on here. Three of the bastards have been shot, but there's at least one more out there, maybe two. They've got guns, and they've got two hostages..."

"And one of them is my daughter," said Mahood quietly, nodding towards the empty passenger seat.

Bryson was crouching near him and Mahood saw how he froze. The hand in which he was holding a pistol dropped. And with his other he reached over to Mahood and held his shoulder.

"Jeez, Mahood, I'm sorry."

Then, after only a second or two, he said: "Look, Mahood, leave this to us. We're getting back-up any moment..."

He paused to listen, as if expecting at that very moment to hear the distant sound of a police siren. But they heard nothing but the sound of the traffic speeding across the overpass above.

"They'll be here soon," Bryson tried to assure him. "And they're properly armed and able to deal with all this."

Mahood looked him straight in the eye. "You don't understand," he said in little more than a whisper. "My daughter's somewhere out there, in the hands of a gunman... and you want me to just sit here and wait!"

"They're a unit, Mahood. They're trained for this sort of thing."

"Trained, are they? Trained to find black cats in cellars in the middle of the night... are they?"

He nodded at the area of wasteland which stretched out along the motorway on the other side of the roundabout. There was a row of houses well over to the left, several hundred yards away, but between that and the crowded motorway there was nothing but darkness. An unlit lane, lined by low trees, seemed to lead off into this area, and on either side of it Mahood thought he could dimly make out the small huts and fences which indicated a series of allotments. Further away there seemed to be some low buildings, storehouses or depots of some sort.

Mahood took his own gun out of its holster. "I'm going in," he said curtly.

Bryson put a restraining hand on his chest.

"No," he repeated, "leave it to the unit that's coming."

Mahood stared at him, his eyes glazed. Then he pushed past him impatiently.

"If your daughter was in there," he murmured through grated teeth, "would you be able to just sit here and wait?"

Bryson pulled him back and shoved something black and heavy into his hand. "At least," he said, "take this radio with you. So we can keep track of your movements."

Mahood slid it into his coat pocket.

28

Instead of taking the narrow lane into the allotments that Thompson had indicated, Mahood cut quickly across into the shelter of the motorway embankment. Its steep slopes were plunged in thick shadow. But as his eyes accustomed themselves to the gloom, he realised that the phosphorescent lights running along the motorway's central reserve threw a dim orange glow on to the jumbled mass of the allotments. The embankment itself was in shadow. Mahood knew that was his best chance of making his way into the maze of plots undetected. He would follow the deep line of darkness along the fence that divided embankment from allotments. And keep his eyes peeled for any movement among the garden sheds and bean-rows.

He began to move cautiously along the low wire-mesh fence, peering constantly in among the small wooden shacks, the fences and the rows of runner beans. It was difficult to see anything. His view was often obscured by the various climbing plants which curled up and sometimes over the netting of the fence. He went on for what seemed an age. He paused at each of the narrow paths which intersected the allotments, waiting for the fugitive to reveal himself by some injudicious movement or noise. But nothing stirred. There was nothing to see or hear. And as he moved further away from the roundabout, the light grew even dimmer. He could now see virtually nothing.

Some two hundred yards from the roundabout he noticed that half way up the embankment stood a squat rectangle of bricks, an electrical sub-station of some sort, judging by the steady hum from inside. Possibly something to do with the motorway. Whatever it was, it might give him a better position from which to survey the allotment area. He moved cautiously up behind it and looked out across the maze of huts and fences towards the distant row of houses.

He now had a much better idea of the lie of the land. He saw that the narrow lane that led off the roundabout went straight as a die, then did a rapid zigzag and finally came out into an unpaved open space to his right. It was surrounded by a high wire fence, with double gates at the far side. Some sort of rough parking area for lorries, he guessed, though there was no sign of any vehicles. He caught the dull glint of stagnant water. Obviously the recent rain hadn't totally drained from the gravel surface of this open ground.

On the near side of the lorry park, not far from the motorway embankment and only fifty yards from where Mahood was crouching, stood a rectangular portacabin, some sort of mobile office or maybe a watchman's hut. And it was this hut that caught his attention. Though it lay in deep shadow he had the impression that its door, on the side facing him, was open. And then, even as he watched, there was no longer any doubt. A rapid flash of light, a stab of torchlight, came from within, and showed clearly the shape of the half-open door.

He had found them.

Mahood was one of those people who become calmer in a crisis. If his heart was beating fast he was not aware of it. A cool determination took hold of him, telling him he had a task to fulfil. Yes, it involved his daughter, and another man who had been a colleague and companion. But he did not stop to ponder the danger they were in, or the threat to himself. Something had to be done, and he was the only one who could do it. As he slid down the embankment towards the flimsy wire fence, he pulled out his own powerful torch. He always carried it on night duties. He held it, unlit, in his left hand. In his right hand was the revolver.

For several minutes he could find no easy way through the fence. He was now close to the portacabin, and for a moment he thought he heard the low murmur of voices, intense and urgent. Did that mean there were two gunmen after all, discussing their next move? He searched carefully and methodically for some way through the fence. But finding none near the cabin, he was forced to move away, back the way he had come. Finally he found one, a place where two layers of wire netting overlapped, and had been bent aside. Made, no doubt, by some local kids, and just big enough for him to push through his lanky frame. In a moment he was on the other side, and moving back towards the cabin along a verge of rough, tangled grass.

There were no voices now. Everything was dark and silent. Mahood stopped a dozen or so yards from the hut. There were three or four wooden steps going up to a small platform in front of the door. Mahood began to move cautiously towards them.

At the bottom of the steps he paused. Was it a moan he had heard? The traffic on the nearby motorway was still humming, droning, swishing by, so he was not convinced the sound had meant anything. Then, quite suddenly, there was a voice.

"You'll never get away with it, you know."

It was McFaul's voice, low, struggling to be calm, but full of emotion.

The voice that answered it was much higher-pitched, but equally nervous. "F*** you, McFaul. I may never get out of this alive, but if that's the case nor will you. I promise you that... I swear it... on my mother's grave..."

The man broke off. It was not the voice of a thug. It was lightly pitched, more like a boy's voice, and despite the violence of the words it seemed to Mahood it was an educated voice. Not the sort of voice that was used to uttering obscenities.

Mahood now understood two things clearly. Firstly there was only one gunman. And secondly he was in considerable pain. He was finding it difficult to concentrate on what he said. And that made Mahood confident.

"Let the girl go, at least," said McFaul's voice. "She has no part in this."

There was a low, uneven chuckle.

"You think I'm stupid... I bet some of those bastards with guns out there wouldn't hesitate a moment about barging in here if they thought *you* were the only hostage I have. But a girl? A sweet young teenage girl. That's a different matter!"

There was a faint whimper, barely audible. But it was enough to confirm that Deirdre was indeed there with them. By the sound of it she seemed to be on the near side of the hut, somewhere near McFaul, not far from the door. What Mahood was absolutely sure of was that the gunman was facing the door. His voice came clear and crisp, whereas McFaul's was just slightly muffled. All three seemed to be sitting, or perhaps kneeling, on the floor.

That made things more difficult. The gunman would have the door covered, as well as his prisoners. The hut was in total darkness, which made it all the riskier. If Mahood tried to rush in and surprise him, he would be silhouetted against the door. The man could easily pick him off, and get off at least one more round, taking one or other of the hostages. Mahood couldn't take that chance.

It was at this point that things began to go wrong. Mahood had forgotten the radio he had stuffed in his pocket. Suddenly it burst into life. A muffled, crackling voice shattered the silence.

"Control to Mahood. Where the hell have you got to?"

Damn it! He'd forgotten to switch the damned thing off. He grabbed in his pocket and flicked off the switch, but it was too late.

"You see," McFaul's voice came, "they've surrounded you already. It's time you gave up..."

"Shut your face! There's only one guy out there... And as you heard, he's lost! They don't know where he is... Hey, you out there! If you come anywhere near that door I'm going to get rid of your friend in here! You understand?"

Mahood moved away from the door, then replied as calmly but as clearly as he could: "I understand... But my friend is right. It's hopeless to try to get away. The area's totally surrou..."

"Shut up!" the man screamed again, and there was a sharp crack and in the dim glow of the motorway lights Mahood saw a hole had appeared low in the plasterboard of the door, not six inches from where he had just been crouching.

There were several endless moments of silence. Mahood found that at the sound of the shot he had fallen flat on to his stomach, the gun in his hand trained on the door. Somewhere, a long way away, he could hear the faint throbbing of a distant helicopter.

"Hey, you!" came the voice from inside. "The man with the two-way. Tell your bosses these people are going to die unless I get an escape car..."

"There's no way they're going to give…" McFaul began.

"Shut up!" the man screamed again. "Hey, two-way man! Did you hear that? Get on to your walkie-talkie and tell them I'm not going to give myself up unless…" His voice trailed off, and again Mahood though he heard a low moan. Then there was some muttering.

"Look," shouted Mahood. "You need to get to a hospital. We can help you. But before that, just let the girl come out. If you like I'll come in instead of her. But let her out… She's innocent of…"

There was another loud crack and again splinters flew out of the cabin's flimsy plasterboard wall. The gunman was evidently trying to find Mahood by the sound of his voice.

The drone of the helicopter was getting louder. Perhaps it's coming here? Mahood thought, but immediately dismissed the idea. How could a helicopter help in this kind of situation?

"Hey, you out there… are you still alive?"

"Yeah, I'm here…" Mahood replied, and immediately moved his position, just in case.

"Maybe I'll do a deal with you…"

At this point Deirdre's voice cut in. "Daddy, don't do a deal with him. Don't put yourself in danger…"

There was a third shot.

Mahood's mouth literally fell. He went numb with fear and shock. But a moment later there came the sound of stifled weeping from the corner he had identified as his daughter's.

"That's just to warn you, girly," came the young man's voice, "to keep your mouth shut. I'm dictating the rules at the moment. So don't forget it…"

Then he raised his voice. "So Big Chief outside is your father, eh? So he won't want a hair hurt off your head, will he? Hey, mister! Mr. policeman if that's what you are. Do you want to come in here? If you come in, nice and quiet and all, I just might be willing to talk about letting your daughter go... But you have to come in first, mind! And unarmed. You've got a gun, haven't you? I want you to throw it in the door..."

The helicopter was now much closer, evidently heading up the motorway.

"How do I know you won't just shoot me, for the hell of it?" Mahood called, and moved again.

"Well you'll just have to trust me on that one, won't you? You in return for your little daughter here - you can't get fairer than that."

Suddenly the helicopter was upon them, quite literally. It wheeled overhead, and a brilliant searchlight split the darkness, playing here and there over the allotments, obviously searching.

'Damn them!' Mahood said to himself. 'What do they think they're playing at?'

The man was shouting something from inside, but Mahood couldn't hear what it was. He shouted something back, but it was hopeless. Their voices were drowned by the whirring, beating, roaring of the giant metal bird overhead.

Then Mahood thought he heard another shot inside the cabin. He was not absolutely sure, because of the noise of the helicopter. But he thought he heard it, and he knew at that instant he could wait no more. The beam from the helicopter swung rapidly across the pitted ground of the lorry park and was suddenly on them, bathing everything in a lurid, blinding light.

Mahood took his chance. He leaped forward up the steps and kicked the flimsy door aside, aiming his gun at the spot where he was convinced the gunman would be lying...

But the man wasn't there. He had moved across to his prisoners, and was trying to drag McFaul to his feet. Mahood fired, but missed. At the same moment the gunman released McFaul's arm and fired back.

How Deirdre came to be in the way Mahood could not understand. At the moment it happened or afterwards. Maybe she had made a quick dash for the door. Maybe she just got in the way in the confusion.

Maybe she had been trying to shelter him from the bullet.

He would never know, because when she fell into his arms she was probably already dead.

29

Mahood had taken to going out to the end of the mole, climbing on to the sea wall and exposing himself to the fierce west winds, watching the waves crash against the big stones below. It was almost as if he wanted the waves and the wind to cleanse him, blow away the dark feelings and wash away the guilt that haunted him constantly now. And indeed it sometimes did seem to help. Somehow, when he turned and walked back to the house, he felt calmer, though it was possible, he sometimes told himself, that it was just that the raw edges of his emotions had been numbed by the elements.

He had reached the main street and turned left past the pub when he saw them coming several hundred yards away, mother and son, side by side.

Why, Mahood wondered later, had he not crossed the road to speak to them? He had wanted to have a good talk with Kathleen ever since the day on the mountain. There had been something left unsaid between them, he felt. An apology, maybe, or at least an explanation.

Kathleen was walking head down as usual, in her normal state of preoccupation, hardly seeming to bother about the shock-haired boy who had trailed some way behind her, kicking at something in the gutter. She turned for a moment to let him catch up. Then seemed to give up, and turned round again to resume her steady, ponderous walk along the pavement.

A woman stepped out of the bakery and engaged Kathleen in conversation. Tony drifted round the two women, continuing to kick at various pieces of paper on the pavement. Mahood continued along his own side of the street, until he was nearly opposite. Kathleen had her back to him. Should he go over and greet them? What sort of response would he receive?

Tony looked up and saw him. But Tony was so short-sighted that he clearly wasn't quite sure who it was standing there across the street.

Mahood raised a hand in greeting, but the boy merely went on staring at him... or past him, he wasn't sure. Kathleen, all the while, still had her back to him.

Something was urging Mahood, very strongly, that this time above all others he should go over and say something. You might not get another chance, it said. But immediately another voice derided the prompting of the first. You'll embarrass her in front of the other woman, it said. You can go and see her and Tony later in the day, at their house, or tomorrow, or the next day. You have all the time in the world to say anything you want to say.

Kathleen finished talking with her friend, and turned to continue her way along the street. She didn't look his way. Tony trotted after her, his head still turned in Mahood's direction, as if still trying to make out if it were 'the Man' or not. He said nothing to his mother. Had she perhaps spotted Mahood after all, and decided to avoid him? There was nothing in her manner to suggest this. But if it were the case, it would be all the more foolish running after her just to say hello.

The things he had to say were complicated. They needed careful wording and a lot of thought.

He turned away, continuing along the street to where it turned up towards the car park on the headland and the sharp turn to the right towards Maeve Meehan's shop.

But he had only gone a few steps when he stopped, suddenly filled by an inexplicable wave of emotion. Mahood had never been a nervous man. He had never been given to panic attacks. But that one moment in his life he experienced what he could only describe as a wild, searing pain of nostalgia and regret. It was as if all the stab wounds which fate had rained down on him that past year suddenly returned in one powerful, stinging blow, and pierced right through to his heart.

He wanted to go running back along the road, to speak to the only person who might have understood that he was not raving mad.

But it was far too late now. Kathleen and her son had long since disappeared from the empty street.

30

The van drove up out of the village, past Mulligan's pub, past the fish packing plant and the road down to the harbour, up to the car park on the first headland and round the corner towards Maeve Meahan's. Tony glanced up to the left, towards the big house.

The man's car wasn't there.

Where could he be?

Tony felt a sudden surge of panic. Had something happened to him already?

Or would the man come back? Might there still be time to warn him, if he could just persuade his Mam to stop?

She saw he was agitated and said, looking down at him: "He's not there, your friend. Father Brian said he went off somewhere this morning, so we won't be able to call and say goodbye."

She sensed that he was disappointed, and put her arm round his shoulder.

Yet Tony's feelings were more complicated than that, and he was still having difficult sorting them out. Yes, in a way he was disappointed he would miss saying goodbye to the man. And he also felt guilty at what he had done to the man's shed. Yet he was also still angry, angry that the man had told lies to Constable Flanagan about what had happened on the mountain. Angry that the man was involved in something with the other man they had met there, and had not been honest enough to tell him or his mother the truth about it.

Angry, above all, because the man had evidently thought that he, Tony, was so stupid he couldn't understand that there was something sinister going on there. Angry because the man had counted on everyone believing his own version, and not Tony's. Because Tony, as everyone knew, was stupid.

That, Tony felt, was the worst betrayal.

Yet he would miss the man. He was the only one who had seemed to understand why he drew the magic signs.

They were now passing the gate that led up to the "Bastion". The big house stood on the brow of the hill, empty and forbidding as always. Tony felt its hostility. It was looking straight at him. The man needed to be warned. That house would get him. He needed to leave at once.

But they were past it already and sweeping on up the hill. Round another corner and along a short straight, and you could look down again at the house. It was still staring at him with a hostile, provocative stare. As if it had won some victory. Tony felt he had failed. He had not warned the man in time.

They turned the last bend and the house disappeared from view.

Shamie was walking along the shore road towards Killoole. He had almost reached the turn-off into the village when he saw a strange minibus cruising down the upper road from the cross-roads. It slowed for the junction, but then accelerated past him, heading for Donegal town. As it flashed past, he caught a glimpse of a face in one of the windows, the face of Tony Dougherty. The 'little moron', as Shelagh McKeever had always insisted on calling him, was leaving town.

Shamie had been thinking of other things, but the sight of the smudged pale face in the bus window, with the round, owl-like spectacles and mournful expression, left Shamie with an unpleasant feeling in the pit of his stomach. They were taking Tony away. What sort of place would he end up in? Poor cub. He had always been irritating, that was true. Shamie could understand why Shelagh mocked him so much. But he had never done anyone any harm. And he had always been the most pathetically 'loyal' of Shamie's followers, the most unquestioning. In some ways the most reliable.

That one glimpse of Tony's face had produced emotions in Shamie he had never experienced before.

He picked up a stick lying by the road and started aimlessly hacking at the dead ferns which festooned the roadside bank. As he went on his way the swing of his stick became more vehement, and soon he was attacking the half-dead bracken with a ferocity that surprised even himself. He stopped for a moment and looked down at his hand. He saw it was trembling uncontrollably.

It was several moments before he noticed the white van parked in the lay-by just before the junction, not fifty yards away. A man was sitting on the wall near the van, gazing intently out to sea. It was someone he recognised, someone he knew well. Pat, the red-headed barman who had been working at Mulligan's for the last few months.

Shamie had always been afraid of Pat. He couldn't say why. He'd only met him a few times, when he slipped into the bar to find his father or, on that one day, Donal MacManus. But each time Pat had looked down on him with his condescending smile and his green, piercing eyes, it was as if he were trying to see inside Shamie's brain, to find out just what Shamie was thinking. Shamie had decided from the start there was something creepy about him. And when he saw Pat now, sitting on the wall, he hesitated. Then he walked on, quickly. He intended just to say a cheery hello and go straight past. But as he approached Pat signalled to him to come over and join him.

"What is it?" asked Shamie gruffly. "What do you want?"

"Come over and sit with me a moment," said Pat.

"I'll be late for my tea if I don't go on," said Shamie, lying through his teeth. "My Mam's always cross when I'm late for tea."

Pat looked at his watch. "It's only four-thirty," he noted sternly. "Your tea won't be ready for another hour at least."

Reluctantly Shamie went and stood near him.

Pat swung his legs over the wall to face him directly.

"You're pally with Donal MacManus, aren't you?" he said.

Shamie didn't like the look in the barman's eye. His manner was cheerful and friendly enough, but his eyes gave him away. Pat was angry about something. He looked as if he wanted to take it out on someone.

Shamie had never seen him this close up, and all his previous misgivings were confirmed. There was something very weird and scary about this man.

"No, I hardly know Donal at all. Sure no one gets on with Donal. He's always getting drunk and throwing his weight around..."

"But you've paid him one or two visits, haven't you? Told him stuff?"

"What stuff? What would I have to tell Donal about?"

A thin smile came to Pat's face, as if he admired the boy's pluck but knew it would do him no good.

"Certain people," he said, "have overheard conversations between the two of you."

"What are you talking about? What people?"

"Well, me for instance!"

Shamie stared at him.

"At Mulligan's... In the entrance, and then in the bar when you came in? Don't you remember?"

Shamie thought furiously. "But I was just asking him about my cousin Micky... He went off to the North and I heard... he had joined the IRA. They say Donal was in the IRA you know..."

Pat nodded slowly, and a strange smile came to his face. "Yes, I know," he said.

Neither said anything for several moments. Shamie shifted his weight uneasily from one foot to the other, wanting to break away, but finding he couldn't - not, that is, until he received some signal from Pat that he had permission.

"Tell me," said Pat finally, "what do you know, Shamie, about the meetings that Donal has with the man from the big house?"

Shamie looked at him, genuinely surprised. "Meetings? Who told you they had meetings?"

Pat fixed his eyes on the boy like some carnivore hypnotising its prey.

"Nobody told me. I've seen them myself. The man in the house drives out of the village a lot, and I'm sure he meets somebody. You don't know anything about that? It wouldn't be Donal now, would it?"

Shamie shook his head vehemently. "If they drove off from the village I would hardly have seen them," he pointed out. "I can't drive a car."

Pat nodded amiably. "But Donal might have told you something... I've a feeling, for instance, that they've met in a bar near Glendoe. He's never mentioned that to you? After all, you're quite friendly with Donal, aren't you?"

Shamie shook his head a second time. "I never heard him say anything about the man. But he would hardly have known him. Sure they say the man from the big house is from the North, and a Protestant. I've heard say even that he was in the RUC... So Donal wouldn't have anything to do with him, would he!"

Pat had turned his head and was looking out at the broad sweep of the sea. The horizon that day was little more than a misty blur where one grey merged with another.

"Ah, do you think not?" he said quietly.

He said no more, so Shamie made off as quickly as he could.

31

Donal's world was in a spin. He had left his bar stool some time before, uncertain that he would be able to keep his balance, and groped his way through the heaving, laughing crowd to the one free seat he could see, by the window near the bar entrance. Above all he didn't want the humiliation of tottering off a bar stool. He would never be able to live it down if that happened. There was no respecting a man round here if he couldn't hold his drink.

He collapsed thankfully on to the seat by the window. At least he had made it that far. Outside, he noticed, it had stopped raining, though the street still glistened in the harsh glow of the street lights.

In front of him there was a swirl of legs, arms, torsos, hands clutching their glasses, men pushing or swaying to the accompaniment of shouts, laughs, snatches of sentences, and the lone attempt to bring in some harmony, from the solo fiddler at the other side of the room. Donal leant back in the seat and closed his eyes. Ah, just a few minutes to relax, a few moments of peace…

But now he had to go to the gents. Curse it! That meant pushing his way once again through the scrum in the middle of the room. Why had he come here on a Saturday night? Now that the two heavies from Belfast had departed the scene, he could come here any night he liked. And he knew it was always crowded on Saturday. People from all along the coast seemed to come down here to spend their money. Mulligan's was the most popular bar in the village. But that was his weakness now. He just did not feel able to stay by himself, up there at the cottage.

With a heave he launched himself off the bench, knocking against a table and almost overturning the neighbouring couple's drinks.

"Hey, watch it, you eedgit!" came the man's protest, relatively good-humoured because he had only lost a few drops. "Get your ould woman to take you home…" His voice disappeared behind the wall of chatter and song in the middle of the bar. For several moments Donal found himself trapped among the swaying bodies and flailing arms, with an increasing feeling of being hemmed in. But Donal had never been one to allow his way to be blocked. He lurched heavily in the general direction of the gents' loo.

Two of the customers turned angrily on him, one of them wiping the beer from his face.

"What the f*** do you think you're doing?" said the man.

"Go to f*** yourself," said Donal thickly. "Who the f*** invited you here anyway?" The man was not local. Donal would have known him if he was.

Suddenly Pat the barman was by Donal's side, clutching him by the arm. "Donal," he said, "I think you've had enough for tonight, brother."

Donal looked him straight in the eye, and was about to throw off Pat's grip on his arm. But there was something about the barman's pale face and steely eyes that made him hesitate.

"Just goin' to the gents'...," said Donal submissively. "And this gawbeen knocked into me..."

There were further protests from around him, but Pat eased him away from the offended parties and towards the toilet entrance.

"Go and do your business," said the red-haired barman in a low voice, "and if you have any sense, don't come back inside. Away off to that cottage of yours and sleep it off... You can get out through the yard."

Donal was about to protest, but again saw the look in Pat's eyes. He pushed clumsily into the passage that led to the gents. As he tottered unsteadily along it, he wondered vaguely how Pat knew where he lived...

Should he go home? He had been generally thinking about it before the barman's intervention, but now he wasn't so sure. Who the hell was this red-headed bastard half his age, telling people what they could and couldn't do? He made up his mind to go back into the bar...

Only now, after relieving himself, he suddenly felt much worse. He had a splitting headache, and he knew that it would not be long before he threw up.

Donal saw a door that he presumed led into the back yard, and pushed it open. It was a much narrower space than he had expected, and cluttered with metal beer barrels and at least two vehicles. It had begun to rain, and a fierce gust of wind rushed up the alleyway from the street, catching at Donal's shabby fleece.

Maybe it was the effect of the fresh air, but Donal found he just couldn't hold on any longer. He steadied himself against one of the vehicles and suddenly it came... He began to retch like mad and vomited all over the side of the vehicle...

A few minutes later, when it had all finished, he opened his eyes. The headache had eased, but all round him there was a terrible stench from his own vomit. He stumbled away from it, and as he did so he looked up to see if he recognised the vehicle he had desecrated...

Even in the dim light of the yard he could see that it was white. It was one of those square, white vans that people curse at when they sweep past you on bends...

The sort of van that had followed Donal along the road to Glendoe.

Donal knew at once he had to get home.

32

"After Deirdre died," Mahood told the priest. "I held myself together long enough to get through the funeral."

They were sitting by the great fireplace in the sitting room, watching the flames lick round the pile of turf in the grate. Every so often the flames guttered and sank back into the deep brown slabs as a gust of wind pushed its way down the chimney. They were both holding the obligatory whiskey.

"They covered up the fact that Deirdre died in the Baird kidnap attempt. Kept it from the papers. The Chief Constable said it was to help me – and maybe it was in a sense. But I don't think that was the main reason. It was to prevent morale in the force from dropping. You know… senior officer couldn't prevent his daughter being killed. Wouldn't have looked good in the papers."

"But some people knew. People in the force. And I know what some of them thought. Same as the papers would have said. 'Silly bugger couldn't save his own daughter. Probably got her killed…'"

"I was calm, upright, even polite to the people who flocked to give their condolences. And yet all the time I wanted rid of them. I didn't need them. I wished they would go away and that the whole business would finish as soon as possible."

The day after the funeral Catriona left. She had said virtually nothing to him since it had all happened.

"She went back to Scotland, to her mother's place. You see, for her it was all my fault. I had been there. I had made a mess of things. What had happened had been entirely my fault and no one else's."

'It was your damned pride,' she had said to him, in the one big row they did have, the day before the funeral. *'Your damned stiffed-neck Ulster pride. You thought that you, only you, were good and clever enough to go in and save them, didn't you!'*

She was irrational from grief, he knew. But it had been difficult to take.

'*I went in because my daughter needed help,*' he had told her quietly. '*And I was there, on the spot, before anyone else.*'

'*And If you'd only waited for back-up, as they told you to, if you'd just waited for the experts, the people who know how to handle these things...*'

'*The same would have happened, whoever had gone in.*' That's what all the guys at the station had told him, anyway. But did he quite believe it? Catriona's words had planted the first doubts...

'*Why didn't you bargain? Let him take McFaul and get him to give back your daughter... our daughter? Oh no, you had to do your duty! You had to put your own interests last... but you forgot that there were other people involved. Other people going to suffer for your pig-headedness! Us! Me and Deirdre...*'

He had simply left the room. Gone to his study and locked himself in. But she had come and banged on the door, her voice growing more hysterical by the minute.

'*Stubborn, pig-headed bastard! Useless, incompetent fool! You could have stopped it. You didn't think of us, of me and Deirdre...*'

No matter how much he rationalised it, he knew she wasn't totally wrong.

"Catriona left the day after the funeral, for Scotland. She went early, without saying goodbye."

He had been given a month's leave of absence from the police. But the very day Catriona left he made his decision. He submitted his resignation. He wasn't fit, he felt, either mentally or morally, to continue.

For three days after that he did not leave the house. The phone went and he did not answer. People rang the doorbell. He knew that when it rang insistently it was his friends. But he did not answer.

He hardly ate, but drank coffee continuously. Black coffee after the milk went sour. He felt nothing. There was an enormous void at the centre of his being. The life that continued, for better for worse, outside the seven rooms of his house had no meaning. He could not understand why people went on doing what they were doing - the milkman, the bus drivers, the taxi men, all the people hurrying so urgently to their work. It was all meaningless. Didn't they know?

A vacuum. Nothing there at all. Even the blank wall opposite, with its faded wallpaper, was part of a dream. And yet who had ever experienced such a featureless, empty dream?

He slept, at night, but when he woke again he felt the same dead weight on his life. He got up, made a coffee, sat. Flicked on the television. Switched from one channel to the next, endlessly. Turned it off again. Walked through the house. Sat down again. Turned on the television...

After three days he knew he had to do something. He had to go and buy some food, for a start. But much more than that. He had to do something to give meaning back to his life.

He thought of revenge. But against whom? The man who had killed his daughter was himself dead. Mahood couldn't remember shooting him. But that's what they said he had done. As Deirdre fell on him.

The more he thought about it, the more he was convinced they had got it wrong. He could not have pulled the trigger... Deirdre had been between him and the gunman.

So who had killed the man? One of his colleagues who burst in when they heard the shot? McFaul, perhaps?

He didn't really care. Even if the man had been alive, Mahood felt nothing towards him. Certainly no sympathy, but not much animosity either. Just another kid misled by propaganda who wanted to give meaning to *his* life.

Meaning. Meaning. How could he himself find meaning, now that everything he cared about was gone? But as the hours passed, on that fourth day, he knew with ever greater certainty that he had to find something to latch on to, some goal to give himself, some challenge to overcome and complete.

And he knew with ever greater certainty that he *would* find something, and do it.

It was only then that the huge depression which had held him numb began to dissipate, and he found that the power to do things was gradually returning. The next time the phone rang, he answered it.

"Brian? It's Ivan here. Ivan McFaul. Are you all right, mate?"

Brian? No one ever called him that. Except his wife. To his colleagues he had always been Mahood. And McFaul's familiarity annoyed him. He answered mechanically, but without any warmth, or gratitude. He wanted to forget his previous life, his colleagues, what it had all meant.

He needed something new to do.

And at the end of that day, after no one else had called, he felt the first stirrings of gratitude. The others, having no doubt phoned before and got no answer, had given up on him. Only McFaul had persisted. And he found that McFaul, who had been there with him when it happened, was now the only one he trusted.

"So you decided you needed a new goal?" asked the young priest tentatively. "What sort of thing did you have in mind?"

Mahood gave him an expressionless look.

"I didn't," he said blankly. "I didn't have anything in mind."

Not at first, anyway. But soon, in stark contrast to the listless state in which he had stayed for days, there formed a knot of conviction which almost screamed for action. He had to leave the house he had shared for so long with the two most important people in his life. He had to get rid of it and go somewhere else. But where? Scotland? England? Somewhere far away, like Australia or Canada?

No, that would be running away, and it would make life even more meaningless. It had to be here, somewhere close to where it all had happened...

And then the idea came to him.

He couldn't work out where it came from. It just welled out of the confused jumble of thoughts in his head. But he knew at once that this was it, this was what he *had* to do.

He would go and live among them, the people on the 'other side' that he had grown up to distrust and fear. The side where the gunman had come from. He would live among them, and prove to himself that they were ordinary people like himself, and - more important - to prove to them that he was an ordinary person, just like them.

It would be hard. It might well be impossible. He would be trying to overcome *the* great divide. It would doubtless throw up endless failures and disappointments, as people would inevitably misunderstand his motives and react with suspicion. He would have to do it with circumspection, with cunning even, so as not to arouse suspicion and not be laughed at. He would have to plan, think out every step.

But it was something he could fix on, a worthy goal, not just for the release he knew it would give him, but also for the very reason that it was so complex, so fraught with problems, so endless…

It would be a challenge worth attempting, because of its very difficulty.

But what was it, specifically, that he wanted to achieve? He wasn't sure. Perhaps just to live in the midst of the Catholic community and be accepted. Yes, and accept them. Perhaps that would be enough.

"But I still don't understand why you came *here?*" asked the priest, quietly. "I mean here of all places?" He was clearly not sure what to make of the other man's 'confession'. He had to admit that he *was* still just a mite suspicious of Mahood's motives. Or maybe even of his sanity. "After all, this isn't the North. This isn't the Catholic community you're talking about. We haven't been involved in the strife and the hatred that Northern Catholics have had to go through.

Mahood nodded. "You're right. And in a way I felt I was cheating. This wasn't the full challenge. But that's what I meant about planning, about cunning. This was my first try, an experiment if you like. Somewhere close enough to the North to relate to it, to understand what it was about. Yet not somewhere so embittered that it would make my task hopeless…"

A sudden gust of wind broke against the side of the house…

"So the idea was to give it a try here… and then go back north, as a second stage?" Father Brian's voice betrayed just a touch of scepticism.

Mahood nodded, and there was a hint of amusement even in his own voice. "Possibly. Go back to some village in the Sperrins, or the Glens of Antrim, where they don't really know what a Protestant looks like, and see how that worked…"

"And then finally you would walk into the lion's den - the Falls or Andersonstown?" the normally mild-spoken priest could no longer suppress the irony in his voice.

Mahood gave a dry laugh. "Or perhaps just stay here, or in my Sperrins village. That would be better than being found with a bag over my head and a bullet in my neck in some side street. No, this was my first try… But it's quite possibly going to be the only one."

"Well, you've done quite well so far," said Father Brian in a more relaxed voice. "After all, you've made contact with me… And I'm the arch-enemy, a Catholic priest."

Mahood smiled. "With respect, Catholic priests have never been the enemy. Not to me, at least. In many ways you were my easiest convert."

33

"I'd better get home now," said Father Brian. "But before I do, I'm going to say something one last time… I think it was a mistake to come here. And I think you should leave as soon as possible."

Father Brian had been sitting opposite Mahood, with his back to the window. Behind the dark curtains the frames of the sash windows gave a sharp rattle. The wind was still rising. It would be another rough night.

"And I have to say, in spite of all you've told me, I still don't quite understand why you came here… I mean here to Killoole of all places."

Mahood swirled his whiskey round in the bottom of his glass. The remains of the ice cubes made a pleasant clinking noise. For a long time he didn't answer. He knew that even this man, who in a strange way had become his friend, would not understand.

"Let's just say that I came here once before - a long time ago. And it made a deep impression."

The priest looked at him blankly, then nodded slowly, though clearly he was still trying to interpret the words. "I thought it was something like that… some half-forgotten memory, perhaps, of a better time?" He took a gulp of the whiskey Mahood had pressed him into drinking. Not his drink, really. Not his drink at all. But somehow, on this particular evening, he wanted to keep the man company.

"You will leave, though," Father Brian insisted. "Promise me that."

The amused look returned fleetingly to Mahood's face. "You seem determined to get rid of me," he said. "Why is that? Do you know something I don't?"

Father Brian moved uneasily in the armchair. Almost as if he's squirming, Mahood thought.

"It occurs to me," said the priest finally, "that you haven't made many friends round here. Not friends you could count on…"

"And you don't think there's much prospect of my doing so in the future… Is that it?"

The wind hit the window panes with a sudden thud, as if someone had thrown a sackful of wool against them. It startled even Mahood. He had experienced some wild nights since his arrival, but this one sounded as if it had something special in store.

"No, quite frankly, I don't," said the priest. "And I think you should think of moving, and in the near future."

Mahood gave him one of his searching looks. "Is this about Kathleen Dougherty?" he asked sharply. "You think I have a serious interest in her?"

The priest did not answer, so Mahood went on. "I assure you that it's not true… Maybe you've heard some gossip in the village. But if so, it's just empty gossip… I was sorry for the kid. He's quite a special kid, you know, gifted in ways most people don't appreciate. I also liked him… And I liked his mother. And I felt sorry for them both."

He paused, and for several minutes they listened to the wind gusting strongly round the house, shaking the windows and rattling some distant door upstairs. The warm sitting-room was a haven of tranquillity and calm in a world ruled by ghosts and demons.

"I just wanted to help," murmured Mahood.

"No," said the priest quietly in response. "It's not about Kathleen Dougherty."

Mahood pursed his lips. "You do know something that I don't," he murmured.

The priest shook his head. "No, nothing definite. Just call it a feeling, a hunch. There are strangers in the village. And the atmosphere has suddenly changed. I can feel it in people's words, in the way they look at me. In the way they tell me their confessions. People are behaving strangely. And it's put the fear of God into me."

Mahood glanced at Father Brian. He had his face turned away from the lamp and the red glow of the fire was not enough to reveal his features with any clarity. The conflicting sources of light conspired somehow to give his expression a confused and ambiguous look.

"No, there's something more than that, isn't there?" Mahood insisted.

Father Brian said nothing. The firelight flickered on the priest's face, reflecting, it seemed, the conflict within. Several minutes passed before he finally spoke.

"There is something, but I'm not at liberty to tell you the details..."

"Ah, a secret of the confessional..."

"No, it wasn't told to me in confession." The young priest smiled. "In fact it's probably many years since... my source said confession. No, it's just that things were said to me... in confidence. That's the only way I can put it. But I trust this source. I really think they know what they're talking about. You are... in real danger."

Mahood nodded slowly. Then he got up and went to a desk at the other side of the room. He brought back a slip of paper and handed it to Father Brian.

The priest straightened out the crumpled piece of newsprint and read:

"*McFaul* - *In loving memory of Ivan Peter McFaul, beloved husband to Tanya, devoted father of Jason and Sharon, brother of James and Elizabeth, killed in the line of duty September 15th.*

Ivan, we love you and miss you.

'Blessed are they who die in the Lord.'"

Father Brian passed it back to Mahood.

"Who was he?" he asked gently. "A friend of yours?"

"Yes, he was a friend. And my guardian. He was the one that saved me and Tony and Kathleen on the mountain."

The priest took several moments to digest this.

"And now... he's dead himself. Was it linked to what happened on Slieve Trascart?"

Mahood shrugged. "Maybe. Who knows? McFaul and I had our share of enemies among the loyalists..."

"So it was them…"

"Who knows?" repeated Mahood. "Who knows?"

The embers of the fire stirred in the grate and Mahood leant forward to throw on another turf.

"Do you want me to stay here this night?" asked Father Brian. "I could just sit here by the fire…"

Mahood laughed. "You mean, as my protector? I don't think, with all due respect, that if the guys that are after me are loyalists they'll be scared away by a priest." He chuckled. "They might see it as a bonus, in a way, killing a traitor and a priest in one go…"

"Oh I don't think the guys that are after you are all loyalists," said Father Brian grimly.

Mahood looked up at him sharply. Then slowly he eased himself back into his armchair.

"Have another whiskey," he said.

34

The knock came at three in the morning. Father Brian had left at about half past one, but Mahood had remained by the fire, staring at the embers. He had thought of turning on the television, but knew he would not settle to watching anything. He had played with the idea of taking the car out for a run, just to burn off excess nervous energy. Or maybe to go on driving, to escape and never come back. But it was turning into another unpleasant night, with the rain beginning to drive in squalls against the window panes of the room where he sat. He was reluctant to leave the warmth and comfort of the old house which, for better for worse, had become his home.

The knock came again.

Mahood turned off the sitting room light and through the side window tried to gain a glimpse of who it was standing under the porch, hunched against the rain. But it was too dark, and the figure was just a faint blur of darkness on a background of further darkness. Then he heard a voice, and it seemed to be calling him by name.

He went out into the hall. The light there was off, and he could see the figure on the porch dimly through the frosted glass of the front door. It called again.

"Mr Mahood, are you there? I saw a light on…"

Mahood threw the door open and there was Flanagan, the local Guard.

"Ah, so you *are* there!" said Flanagan. His manner seemed none too friendly. "Can you put on a coat and come with me? I've something to show you."

"At this time of night? Can't it wait till the morning?"

"Put on a coat. I need your advice and your expertise."

Mahood hesitated. What did the man mean, his expertise? If there was police work to be done, he had no jurisdiction here.

"Well are you coming, or not?" asked Flanagan.

Mahood took his raincoat and a cloth cap off a peg near the door and went out with the policeman.

To his surprise Flanagan did not have his car. He set off on foot down the gravel lane towards the road. Mahood followed, wondering where they were going.

Flanagan led him down to the gate, then strode purposefully up the main road for two hundred yards until they came to an untarred lane leading off to the right. Here it became so dark that the policeman had to switch on his torch in order to follow the rough road leading up through the stunted trees. Somewhere ahead there was the noise of a car moving slowly, then stopping. The Guard strode relentlessly onward. After another hundred yards the trees opened out, and Mahood noticed there was a cottage to the left. Flanagan headed in this direction, pushing open a simple wooden gate that led into a roughly paved yard. They could now see a faint light in one of the cottage windows.

A figure suddenly loomed out of the dark in front of them. Flanagan flashed his light towards it, and caught the startled features of Father Brian, the parish priest.

"Oh it's you, Father," said Flanagan. "You should have made your presence known."

"I'd just parked over there," said the priest, "and was making my way to the house. What in God's name has happened here?"

The policeman said nothing, but led the way up the steps that led to the door. He pushed the door open and stood back for them to enter.

The door gave directly on to a plainly furnished room, lit by an unshaded light bulb. To one side the fire was smouldering in an old-fashioned kitchen range, and on a table in the middle of the room were the remains of a simple meal – a half-empty blue-and-white mug, and a plate which still held some potatoes and gravy. Next to the plate was a large, almost full bottle of whiskey.

On the far side of the room, sitting on the floor and propped up against the wall, was a man. Mahood recognised him at once as Donal MacManus, the man he had met at the regatta, and then again on the night of the fire. He recalled how the man had stared at him that night in such a curious way. A look of fear and mistrust, and yet of curiosity. And he remembered the man's warning.

Mahood knew at once that Donal was dead. His eyes stared emptily towards the table, and across his chest there was an enormous patch of red. There was also blood on the floor beside him, a thick pool of dark red liquid. He must, Mahood reckoned, have been dead for several hours.

"It took me some time to find him," Flanagan explained. "Maeve Meahan, down on the main road, was sure she heard a shot and insisted I find out if something had happened. But she wasn't sure which house it had come from exactly..."

Father Brian crossed himself, and knelt down beside the body.

"Don't touch anything, Father," said Flanagan. "You know you mustn't touch anything."

"Lord preserve us," was all that the priest could say. Then he made the sign of the cross over Donal, bowed his head and seemed to lose himself in prayer.

"Why have you brought me here, constable?" Mahood asked. "You obviously know that I'm a detective, but I have no jurisdiction here... You'll have to wait for your colleagues."

Flanagan gave him a cool look. "Yes, I know that," he said, "and that's not why I brought you here. I brought you here to show you what you've done to this village."

"Me? What has this to do with me?"

"It has everything to do with you. Or are you so innocent and unaware that you don't know that the men who did this will be coming after you too? You're next on their list!"

Mahood's eyes narrowed. "How do you work that out?" he asked, his hackles beginning to rise. He didn't believe a word of what this village boor was telling him.

Father Brian stood up and said to him gently: "Mr Flanagan's right, at least as far as your safety's concerned. He was wrong to blame you, Mr Mahood, but please, please, if I were you I'd go now. Back to your house. And pack, and just leave."

There was pain and regret in the priest's voice. Mahood looked at
him, and then at the grim, unsmiling face of the Guard. And then slowly
he nodded.

He held out his hand to the priest. "Thank you, Father Brian. You
are... a true Christian."

"Go in peace," was all Father Brian could say. Then he turned back to
the figure on the floor.

Mahood left the cottage and made his way back down the lane, into
the trees. The rain had stopped for the moment, but all around he heard a
heavy dripping, and the unsettling noise of the wind stirring the branches.
Everything here was dark, and he had no torch. Part of the way along
the lane he panicked and thought he had wandered from the track. A wet
branch brushed across his face...

But finally he emerged on to the main road. The street lights of the
village glowed faintly down to his left. But here there was practically no
light at all. He was able to follow the twisting road only by the faint glow
reflecting off its wet surface. Now he could see the single light, away to
the left, on the telegraph pole above the car park at Maeve's. And ahead of
him, on its lonely promontory, the dim shape of his own house.

He reached the gate which separated his drive from the road and went
through it. His car was parked on its space outside the front door. Vaguely
he wondered if he should not just get in and drive off at once. He had the
keys in his pocket, he realised, and there was nothing to stop him doing
that. But then he decided that this was silly. He would go in and pack a
few things to take with him. The rest he could recover later. Or send for
them.

He let himself into the house, and without switching on the hall light
he crossed to the bottom of the stairs. He knew the house well enough
by now to find his way about in the dark without too much difficulty.
He began to climb the stairs. And then stopped, as he thought he heard
something above.

He listened again, and decided it was just the normal creaking of
the gables in the wind. He continued upwards, and came to the landing.
Fumbling around in the darkness, he found the handle to his bedroom.

Here he had to switch on the light momentarily, to take stock of where everything was. Almost at once he switched it back off again, and headed to the chest of drawers which held most of his clothes. The rest was easy. His hold-all was under the bed and he had no problem fetching it out. A few shirts, pants, socks. Pyjamas. Then out on to the landing again and into the bathroom, to pick up his shaving things.

When he came out he glanced for a moment along the bare landing which led straight to the strange, semi-circular window looking out over the sea. He stopped abruptly in his tracks. It was a dark night, so he couldn't understand why the green and red pattern in the middle of the glass should stand out so clearly. It seemed to be giving off a curious glow that filled the corridor with an eerie light. Then it faded slowly, only to revive again a few seconds later. And fade again.

He had never noticed what the pattern was before. Now he saw clearly that it was a simple picture of an apple, surrounded on three sides by leaves.

What was lighting the window in this strange, unnerving way? It must, he decided, be a distant lighthouse, one he had never noticed before, flashing its warning to any ships unfortunate or foolish enough to be out on such a wild night.

He shook himself and headed to the top of the stairs. Soon he was padding gently downwards, gripping the hold-all in one hand. At the door to the sitting room he stopped. Then he opened it and looked into the darkened room, for one last glance at the place where he had gone through so many emotions over the last few months, which had been the scene of his grief and despair, but also his times of resolve and recovery. A place that had given him some comfort where there was none before.

Then he closed the door again and let himself out of the house.

The rain had started again. He slid into the driving seat and with only the side lights on eased the car down the drive to the gateway. Blast! he thought. I should have left the gate open. Now I'll have to get out of the car again.

The gate swung open with its normal creaking complaint. Then he was back in the comfort and shelter of the car, and driving out. He turned left up the hill, away from the village. He decided to leave the gate open. As a signal to the villagers that their unwelcome guest had gone.

Only now did he switch on the headlights. Without them he could not have negotiated the twists and turns of the climb away from the village. Soon he was at the crossroads above the village.

He turned right, heading along the coast road towards Donegal town.

He suddenly realised, as he moved into top gear, that in a strange way he would miss the village. No one there, not even the priest or Kathleen, had made him fully welcome. He had experienced some things which he could have done without: the shooting on the mountain, the arson attack, now finally the killing of Donal MacManus. But from a distance, from his bleak vantage point on the headland, he had watched the people of the village. And in a strange way warmed to them.

And he had made one friend, for a while, the small, ugly boy who took such pleasure in forming the incomprehensible characters of a far distant civilisation...

Beyond the village the road dropped back towards the coast. He was now approaching the lay-by on the right where tourists liked to stop to look out over the village...

It had been here, such a long time ago, that he had stopped with Catriona and Deirdre to look for the mysterious mountain which hid the place where the sun went into the sea.

Tonight everything was dark and cold. Beyond the wall on his right was the sea, and though it was hidden by the darkness, he could imagine it rolling and tossing angrily as its waters drove relentlessly on to the shore.

The lay-by was now coming up on his right, the seaward side. To his surprise he saw there was a vehicle parked there, with its lights on. As he approached, the car pulled out and attempted to do a U-turn across the road in front of him. He slowed, sure that the car wouldn't make it on the first attempt.

The car had stopped, as he guessed it would, sideways across the narrow road. Mahood pulled to a stop and flashed, to signal he would wait while the car's driver made another attempt to turn. The other car, however, remained stationary across the road, blocking the way forward and the way into the lay-by.

Too late, Mahood realised this was no chance manoeuvre. The car had deliberately barred his way. The road was too narrow to do a U-turn himself. Calmly he put the car into reverse and edged back up the road in the direction he had come from.

Out of the darkness behind him there loomed another vehicle. It must have been following him but had not had its lights on. It too turned and parked sideways across the road. A white van with muddy sides.

And traces of vomit near the driver's door.

35

On the last day of their holiday they had gone back to see the Falling Mountain.

The sun was already beginning to set when they stopped at the little lay-by just before the village. They got out of the car and walked to the wall, the three of them. Deirdre sat on a wooden style that led down to the beach and her parents stood beside her.

"It *is* a falling mountain, Daddy," she exclaimed with satisfaction. "You can see how it's leaning over the sea and about to fall into it."

Her mother smiled, and her father put his hand on her shoulder.

"I hope it's not going to fall just yet," he said, laughing. "It would make quite a splash, and send a wave which would flood the whole village!"

"Poor people," said the girl.

This time it was her mother who laughed. "It's not going to happen, dear," she said. "Your father's imagination runs wild sometimes."

The village, poking out into the sea in front of them, was a dark silhouette against the blazing light of the sunset, the uneven line of its roofs and chimneys forming a neat line between light and darkness. It could have come from a picture in a book. As the gulls wheeled over the little port it all looked so peaceful. You could never imagine anything bad happening there.

Beyond was the hazy outline of the mountain itself, basking in the magical glow of the evening sunshine. It seemed so near, and yet so tantalisingly distant.

"It's a magical mountain, isn't it, Daddy? It has hidden treasures, and monstrous beasts living in great caves, to guard them."

He nodded.

"Yes, my love, I'm sure you're right."

Deirdre's mother turned and walked away, back along the road they had come, humming to herself. Father and daughter went on looking towards the mountain.

"We won't be able to go there today either, will we, Daddy?"

"No, my love, it's too late now. We spent too much time on the beach. By the time we got there it would be almost dark."

"But we've seen it at least, close up, we've seen the Falling Mountain…"

"We have, and we'll never forget that, shall we?"

The girl shook her russet curls.

"No, we'll never forget it," she said emphatically. "And one day, maybe after many years, we'll come again. And next time we'll go there, and climb it, and find out its secret… And we'll see what's on the other side, where the sun goes into the sea."

"Yes, my love, some other time…"

He screwed up his eyes against the setting sun.

"In a different life."

E N D

Made in the USA